THE SISTA HOOD

THE SISTA HOOD

ON THE MIC

A Novel

E-FIERCE

ATRIA BOOKS

New York   London   Toronto   Sydney

ATRIA BOOKS

1230 Avenue of the Americas
New York, NY 10020

Library of Congress Cataloging-in-Publication Data
E-Fierce
    The sista hood : on the mic / E-Fierce.—1st Atria Books pbk. ed.
        p. cm.
ISBN-13: 978-0-7432-8515-5
ISBN-10:   0-7432-8515-8
    1. Puerto Rican women—Fiction. 2. Rap musicians—Fiction. I. Title.

    PS3605.F54S57 2006
    813'.6—dc22

                                                    2006042778

First Atria Books paperback edition July 2006

10 9 8 7 6 5 4 3 2 1

ATRIA BOOKS is a trademark of Simon & Schuster, Inc.

For information regarding special discounts for bulk purchases,
please contact Simon & Schuster Special Sales at 1-800-456-6798
or business@simonandschuster.com

Manufactured in the United States of America

For the ones like THE SISTAHOOD:

the *antepasados* no longer with us,

the grandmothers that sacrificed,

the mothers that resisted,

the aunts that rebelled,

the sisters that challenged and still loved,

the nieces that gave us hope

and the friends that were fierce enough to stay.

THE
SISTA
HOOD

CHAPTER 1

MY WEAPON IS THE MIC

I wanted more than anything in the world to be an emcee. Oh, and to be with Ezekiel Matthews. So, as I rode the San Francisco Muni bus from my wealthy public school neighborhood of St. Francis Wood to my working-class barrio—the Mission—I dreamed. I thought of better times that have passed and of dreams to come. A time when I'll have my own stage, a record deal and my honey on my arm. For now, I'll settle for making it through the next four years of high school.

I opened my sketchbook that Papi gave me for my twelfth birthday. It's worn, like a comfy pair of shoes. It has been loved and plastered over with album covers from my favorite hip-hop artists like Tupac, Missy Elliott, Goapele, Flakiss and Mystic.

I haven't seen Papi in three months. Writing is my way of shouting him out, drenching myself in his light. I just wrote on the bus. Tuned out the noise. Didn't care about the teenage boys that smelled of sweat or the girls that wore clothes so tight their pants would probably rip if they sat down too quickly. I created my own cipher, and wrote as if each word I penned would somehow bring Papi back into my life.

> *I make the most of what I got*
> *Hoping I can blow the spot and make a knot.*
> *But keep my soul intact*
> *If I make it*, Mami, *I'll be back.*

"Yo, why you always gotta be so tough?" Ezekiel said, stretching his neck over my seat to peep my lyrics. "They sound like a dude wrote them. I thought you Latinas were suppose to be soft and sexy and bring me tortillas for lunch?"

"I'm not Mexican. Besides, Puerto Ricans don't eat tortillas," I said as I slammed my notebook closed. I wanted to reply with a cool-ass comeback. Instead, I just sat there like a mute. All I could do to avoid his sexy charcoal-colored eyes was to look out the Muni bus window and chew on my cuticles. Shit, I'm never at a loss for words unless I'm sitting next to MC EZ, as he's known to all his fans in Frisco. I felt both excited to see him and resentful that he had to show up, at the exact moment when I wanted just to be alone.

"I heard this dope rapper once say, 'When society tries to silence us, our most powerful weapon is the mic,'" EZ said. "Which also means how you say it is as important as what you say. That's why you need a serious attitude adjustment, Mari, and stop trying to sound so hard!"

"Hip-hop class is over, and I don't need you to play teacher no more."

"I wasn't dissin' your words, I was tryin' to help a li'l sistah out."

Here I've been dying to see Ezekiel for months, and the first thing he did was criticize me. Forget that he called me li'l sistah, we spent the best eight weeks of my life together this summer. At camp, when I would bust out lyrics about women being strong and smart, he was the only guy who didn't avoid me afterward. All the other guys would be sweating the girls who were more flirtatious and less in-your-face with their rhymes. It's always hard with guys 'cause my steelo could never be some J. Lo or Lil' Kim type, who hooches out and downplays their smarts for the bling-bling.

"Oh, so now you're not talkin' to me?" he said. But I could tell he wasn't mad 'cause he said it as if he were trying to make amends. Maybe he's already tired of his new hottie, J-Ho. Actually her name is Jessica Hoffman. Since she dug her claws into him, brotha man all but disappeared. I might be lovestruck, but I still need to make him earn a sistah's love.

"You haven't spoken to me in five months and suddenly expect everything to be cool?" I said.

"That's not fair, Mariposa, you know I got a lot going on with Jessica, family, church, friends, hip-hop and now school."

He had to go there first with Jessica. I just don't get what he sees in her. Jessica can't even carry on a conversation with herself, let alone relate to what Ezekiel must go through as a Black man in America. She just wants to be Black. Especially after telling me this summer that "he had never been able to relate to a girl like me." Sure, J-Ho gets mad props at school for her rapping skills, but it can't hurt that she's willing to show lots of skin and flaunt her ass in those skintight pants. The dudes love that shit. He probably stays with her 'cause she gives it up easy.

"Well, you could've at least given a sistah a call," I said.

Ezekiel nodded, shifting in his seat. For the first time, he moved away from me. "I will." He sat there without taking his eyes away from mine.

As the sun from the bus window pressed down hot and hard on his *café sin leche* skin, all I could think about was how fine Ezekiel was as he extended his arm behind me along the backside of the seat with such confidence.

Here we were traveling through the Sunset neighborhood of San Francisco—with a man talking to himself in one corner, a White lady clutching her purse close in the other and a bunch of kids talking smack—and Ezekiel just sat there like he belonged. I wanted so badly to be inside his heart, to feel protected by his warmth. I suddenly had this urge to lean over and kiss his nice full lips.

"Oh shit, here comes Fat-Boy," said Ezekiel, turning away from me as he noticed his homeboy enter the bus. They pounded fists.

"What up, EZ?" said Fat-Boy with the XXX shirt.

"Nothin', B, just chillin' with my li'l sister," said Ezekiel.

I shot the boy a hardcore stare. Ezekiel caught my mug, but didn't say anything. Fat-Boy began to feel the heat and bounced.

"Um, I'll check you later, dawg," he said. He moved to the back of the bus toward his friends, where they started joking.

"That's one bitch I never want to get with, playa—she's fine, but not worth the drama," said Fat-Boy.

They all laughed.

Oh, no he didn't. EZ tried to push me down as I stood up to tell the loser a thing about himself. "You pimply faced, Blimpie-eatin', Big Pun *pendejo*—you're just upset 'cause the only bitch you've ever touched is your mama."

Fat-Boy started to say something else, until EZ just

looked at him. That was enough to make him race back to his seat and stay quiet, even with his friends.

"See what I mean, Mari, you be scaring them boys away."

"It's the best repellent I know for keeping the assholes away," I said.

Ezekiel sighed in frustration. "Girl, if you wanna be an emcee you gotta chill a bit more with people. It helps build your fan base."

"Whatcha tryin' to say? I gotta be sugar and spice and everything nice, so you dudes aren't threatened?"

"Mariposa, I'm just sayin' that you can't roll up on guys all tough like you want to build your street cred. Use your cuteness a little more, it'll take you farther."

"It works for Jessica, but it ain't me. I'm not good at all that fake social stuff. I hate it when dudes be calling me a bitch."

"Oh, but it's okay for you to call someone's mama a bitch?"

"Well, it sounded good and he left me alone, right?"

Ezekiel saw right through me, knowing I would never admit to him that I was wrong. I made it easy for him and he just threw my own words right back at me. Him not sticking up for J-Ho surprised me. I also respected him for not rubbing in my face the fact that Fat-Boy only left me alone 'cause I was with him. Don't get me wrong, I could've held it down with my potty mouth. It's my physical well-being that would have been jeopardized. Call me lucky, but my battles always stayed verbal.

"But this ain't you, though. Listen, Mari, this summer you seemed so free. You were able to just let your rhymes flow."

I kept frowning, and he just looked at me till I smiled. It was all good. Then a crew of hotties from around the way entered the bus with their hiked-up skirts and mile-high boots. They worked the bus aisle, loving that all eyes were on them. All the boys started kickin' game and asking for their digits. Ezekiel couldn't stop staring at this one chick who reminded me of J-Ho except she was Black and sported Alicia Keys extensions.

"Check her out," he said.

Life is just too easy for EZ sometimes. People were always telling him what beautiful eyes he had or salivating over his tall and lean body. Even strangers. Mostly girls. His eyes were light brown, almost green. He always said he thought they looked strange against his dark skin. Ezekiel then looked at his reflection in the window. Checking himself out as if wondering whether or not he was good-looking. Yeah, he knew girls were checking him out all the time—but the pickings were slim at Stanford High, so maybe he just felt desperate and that's why he got with Jessica. Whatever happened to Ezekiel spitting lyrics like, "Black is beautiful. Where's my beautiful Black girlfriend? You're a Black man. You're a warrior"?

I wish he was my *papi chulo* and not hers. I've tried real hard to be just friends. I should be happy. It's my second semester as a freshman at Stanford—the most prestigious public high school in San Francisco. But no, I go to school with a bunch of geeky Chinese kids and crazy White kids who do lots of drugs and talk to me only when they want help with their Spanish homework. Shit, my mom cleans some of their houses and my dad works on their cars. And sometimes in class, I'm reminded by my classmates that the only reason I'm at this school is that they had a shortage of Black and Latino applicants, so they took the smartest of us from the worst schools. After all, it couldn't be that we were really smart. Then, when I try to connect with some of the few Latin and Black kids in the courtyard, I gotta see Ezekiel macking on that skank J-Ho, who isn't even a sistah. Maybe if I was a hoochie, a dope-ass emcee or a senior I could've had a chance with him.

"Do you see me as Black or Latina?" I said.

Ezekiel chuckled to himself. "You're always full of surprises, aren't you?"

"Just answer the question!"

"Well, you aren't one of those White-looking Latinas, but you're not Black either. Still, I don't think your folks would be too excited about you bringing a brotha home," he said.

I guess I shouldn't ask questions when I really didn't

want to know the answer. He had to mention my parents, something I didn't want to think about right now. Being true to my unpredictably predictable nature, I rolled my eyes and was ready to box. "You mean, your folks wouldn't be too happy about you bringing home some Puerto Rican whose parents have thick Spanish accents?"

"Mariposa, don't be putting words in my mouth. If I had issues with Latinos, you and I wouldn't be friends, would we?"

"Be real, Ezekiel. At camp you were always making fun of light-skinned brothas or joking about how Latinos could pass."

"Some Latinos can pass, but not you, Mari," he said, really meaning it. He stopped me dead in my tracks. Reminding me why I wanted him in my life.

"It's probably hard for you being a darker Latina."

He can be a smart-ass most of the time, but for some reason he just gets me. Sometimes he reads me better than I can read myself. And as much as I wouldn't want to admit it to his face, he's right about my folks. If I brought home a brother, my pops would be cool, but my mother would definitely have issues.

"Yeah," I said. "Latinos be hatin' on Black folk and Black folk be hatin' on Latinos. The only place I feel in my zone is when I'm spittin', but then I gotta deal with boys hatin' on me 'cause I'm a girl."

He unzipped his backpack and started rummaging through it. After a moment he came up with a Mickey Mouse Pez dispenser. He searched through it more and came up with a package of cherry and orange Pez.

"Which one do you like?"

"I'll take the orange."

EZ began to eat messily, placing the orange Pez into the Mickey Mouse dispenser.

"Now, open your hand," said EZ, and he generously gave me two to eat. He took a couple for himself and then returned it to his backpack.

"Thanks, EZ." I pulled away, putting the Pez in my mouth. The candy tasted sweet and warm.

"My father gave me that Mickey Mouse Pez for my thirteenth birthday and said he would take my sister Sadie and me to Disneyland. That was about four years ago and we still haven't gone. But I carry it with me everywhere." He smiled and looked at me. "Never know when he's gonna get some time off from work and say, 'Hey Ezekiel, let's take that trip.' "

"You think he ever will?"

Ezekiel shook his head. "Sadie and I are too old now. And everything's changed since he gave it to me. I guess I'll just hold on to it."

"Hoping."

"Yeah," he said. "Hoping."

I savored my Pez, sucking it slowly, thinking about

how nice it was to have a real conversation with Ezekiel again. I wish I could be as open as him, especially about my parents. But nothing came out; instead, I just sat there eating my Pez.

"Listen, when are you gonna hook up with my sister?" Ezekiel said. "She hasn't been too happy lately. She could use some new friends."

"I have friends. Me, myself and I," I said. "No, for real, I do have my friend Liza. She's just been caught up in her boyfriend, Rio."

All of a sudden I regretted not letting him in. I knew there was Liza, but even she's been avoiding me lately. EZ was probably the one person I could trust, and I just kept sayin' the wrong thing. I wish I could tell him about my parents getting a divorce. I know peeps get divorced all the time, but it wasn't supposed to happen to my folks. They loved each other. Then, my dad just bounced with some hoochie who had more cheddar. Now, I come home every day to my mom locking herself in her room and crying. I'm never goin' out like that for no dude. Never. I guess I should just keep quiet and not make it worse.

"Listen, Mariposa, stop pouting. It's not attractive. School can't be that bad."

"I'm not pouting. Don't do that, Ezekiel."

"Do what?"

"Don't make it seem like I'm being a baby. You just don't understand, okay."

"Okay," he said. "Look, I know it must be hard for you that I'm dating Jessica. It's just you're more like a li'l sister to me. You don't have to diss me."

"You're such a jerk," I said.

"When'd *you* get to be such a jerk?" he asked.

Ezekiel was silent. I stared down at my cuticle, which was bleeding now.

"Twenty-fourth and Mission," announced the bus driver over the intercom.

I left without looking back.

If I had stayed with him one second longer, I would've burst into tears. All I wanted was for him to love me back. To see in me what he saw in Jessica. I wanted so badly to live in her skin. She can't even rhyme. Yeah, she won the talent show last year, but that's before I came to this school. How can EZ go for her? I wanted him to love me.

I couldn't keep the tears from streaming down my face. I wished I could run home to my dad so he could make it all better with a look, a word or even a hug. But even he's gone. I guess all men just leave one day and never come back. The bus pulled away and I stole a glance at the back of EZ's head and sighed. I saw my own reflection in the back window and began to question who I was and why I was in this world.

CHAPTER 2

THE CHRONICLES OF J-HO

"Give me the pepperoni pizza with ham and pineapple please," I told Stella the bearded lady, standing behind the counter in the cafeteria of Stanford High School.

"We only got cheese or vegetable pizza, sweet cakes," said Stella.

Decisions are never my thing. Besides, Stanford's cafeteria looked more like a mall food court than a public school lunchroom. If I had gone to my neighborhood school, I would've had an open campus and I could be eating a beef burrito from the local taqueria. Instead, I have to choose between veggie wraps, which are really just sorry-ass burritos, soy burgers and tofu tacos. All the food is healthy, but it has no flavor. Can I have a little culture in this mix? I hate choices. It wouldn't be so bad if my only friend, Liza Ortiz, wouldn't have left me solo to be with her boy toy, Rio. Liza and I have known each other since fifth grade and I always become second fiddle to her dudes.

Stella and I both gave Bethany Doll a disgusted look as she stood in line behind me, sportin' her fresh manicure, dove gray cashmere sweater, Prada bag and shimmering blonde hair. "Umm, I'll have the veggie wrap with pesto," said Bethany Doll, twirling her hair around her finger. Bethany lives in Pacific Heights, which the colored peeps call Pacific Whites, and she would never be caught dead in anything that wasn't designer. Unlike the rest of us, who buy the knockoffs on Market Street from street vendors. She can't go anywhere without her sorority in tow. I get all the blonde bimbettes, but how did Evita Romero with her Spanish accent ever get with all these Wonder Bread White girls?

Bethany then turns to Evita, "Isn't she the one that you told me Sadie can't stop talking about?"

Evita just shakes her head in agreement, then rolls her eyes at me.

Is she talking about Sadie Matthews, Ezekiel's sister? You think of all the people in the school I would at least be cool with Evita and Sadie. In my hood, homegirls usually stick together. I'm quickly learning that at Stanford High different rules apply. Rules that I'm still trying to learn.

"Well, why don't you talk to her. You're both Mexican,

don't you live in the same neighborhood?" said Bethany.

"I'm Nicaraguan, not Mexican. What she is, I couldn't care less," said Evita. "I'll save everyone a seat at the table since I already have my lunch." She couldn't get out of there fast enough and she never once looked me in the eye. So much for lookin' out for your own.

Bethany was clueless to the fact that she got under Evita's skin. "Um, Stella I'm waiting for my veggie wrap," said Bethany with a voice of entitlement.

"Wait until Mariposa gives me her order," said Stella.

"Oh, I'm sorry, Maria, I didn't see you," said Bethany.

I know Bethany saw me. I wanted to rip her a new one, but Stella saved me the trouble. Since I started Stanford High School, the only person I really liked was Stella and, of course, Liza when I saw her. I just didn't seem to fit in with my Ben Davis work pants, tight tee, last season's PUMA sneakers and, as always, my ghetto fabulous attitude.

"I'll have the carne asada burrito," I said, rolling my *r*'s and my eyes at Bethany.

Directing her comment to Stella, Bethany said, "Be careful you don't get any man beard in that wrap. Shouldn't you be wearing a hair net for that?"

Why did she have to go there again and make fun of Stella? She never bothered anyone. It takes courage for a woman to sport a beard. I couldn't do it. But freakin' Bethany didn't have to be so mean.

"Some of us keep it natural. Others spend their parents' money to compensate for what God didn't give them," I said.

Stella laughed as she stroked her beard and handed Bethany her food.

"Here's your burrito," said Stella.

Bethany lost interest in Stella as Ezekiel entered the lunchroom. Girls watched him in hopes that he would say hello. Guys wanted to be his friends, hoping that they too could become girl magnets. As always, he managed to capture the attention and the hearts of everyone in the room.

Addressing her fan club, Bethany said, "There's Ezekiel, the amazing rapper I've been telling you about. Let's go say hi, girls." She and her ducklings made a bee-line toward Ezekiel.

EZ just had this unexplainable charm that could win anyone over. But good luck he's sprung out on Jessica. White girls at this school won't give a sistah the time of day, but enter a good-looking brotha and they love them some chocolate. But given the shortage of Latino and Black men, I wish the White girls would step aside.

Ezekiel stepped onto the cafeteria stage with Mr. Mintz, the school drama teacher. Bethany and company just stood below, waving their arms to get his attention. I swear, at that very moment I wanted to line her up with her ducks and start target practice.

"Excuse me, Stanfordites, I have an announcement to make," said Mr. Mintz.

The students continued to chat, uninterested in what he had to say. Mr. Mintz looked to Ezekiel for help. EZ grabbed the microphone and saved the day for the dorky Mr. Mintz.

"Peace, my peoples," he said. The room went hella quiet in two seconds. He handed the mic back to Mr. Mintz. Ezekiel then just stood there like a guard as Mr. Mintz prepared to speak.

I saw Liza sitting next to her boyfriend Rio. Rio is pretty fine with his half-Mexican, half-white self. Not my type, but I can see why Liza was drawn to him on a physical tip. Somehow he managed to eat his cheesesteak sandwich with one hand and the other he had gripped around Liza's neck. Like she was his possession. Sickening. I noticed there was a seat empty on the other side of Liza and I decided to join them.

"We don't care, Mr. Mintz, don't you get it," yelled Rio. The rest of his stoner crew just threw napkins at the podium when Mr. Mintz wasn't looking in their direction.

I put my tray on the table next to Liza. "Hey Liza, thought I'd join you since it's been two weeks since we've spoken."

"I'm sorry, but—" said Liza, unable to finish her sentence as she was cut off by Rio.

"No, you're not sorry. Tell her the truth," said Rio.

"That is the truth," said Liza.

Rio pulled her head closer to his scrawny chest. Then he pushed his head toward me. "She's had more pressing engagements," he said. Then he high-fived his buddies and they all laughed.

Liza smiled halfheartedly, like it was all show.

"Liza's a big girl, I think she can speak for herself," I said. "Are you all right, Liza? You usually call."

Liza looked away from me. Rio gave her this controlling look that made me want to jump across Liza and just kick his butt.

Liza looked back at me and with this sudden burst of confidence said, "Yeah, I've had better things to do."

"Oh, so it's like that?" A part of me knew deep inside that Liza was fronting. Another part of me was really mad that she would prioritize some dude over our friendship.

Liza hurt my feelings, plain and simple. I could take being ignored or being made fun of by anyone else, but not her. All those times I made my mom let her stay with us when her own mother was being verbally abusive. My own secret thoughts I told her and never trusted anyone else to tell. All the times when I could've chosen to be with the cool kids, but instead stood up for Liza's half-White and half-Filipina ass when the kids in the school yard called her "poor White trash." I took many hits for

Liza, all in the name of friendship. I always thought that's what you did for your homegirls. You defended them in public, and then when you were alone you told them the truth.

I sat there surrounded by people, but I felt small and alone. Bethany and her crew kept jumping up and down to get EZ's attention. EZ winked at me, which somehow eased the pain of Liza's words. Bethany just rolled her eyes at me, then went back to drooling over EZ.

"This year's talent show auditions will happen a week from this Thursday after school. This year we have a special treat, as the winner will attend the Hip-Hop Leadership Camp this summer in Los Angeles, all expenses paid. Our judges will be none other than our own Ezekiel Matthews and . . ."

"Go EZ, go EZ," chanted the students, not really caring about what Mr. Mintz was saying.

". . . And the famous Missy Elliott. I'll post a sign-up sheet on my door after lunch. Now, I'd like to turn the mic over to last year's winner—Mr. Ezekiel Matthews," said Mr. Mintz, gladly giving up the mic.

The crowd went wild. Everyone cheered Ezekiel on as he prepared to work the mic.

Rio then got up and Liza followed as she bussed both of their trays. As Rio was walking off, Liza mouthed that she would call me later. I shook my head that I understood, but knew better than to count on it. Honestly, I missed our afterschool hanging out. I would write songs and she would show me her latest b-girl moves. We won two talent shows in junior high school as MC Patria and Pinay-1. Drowning in this sea of whiteness, I could really use a friend like her.

Enter, J-Ho in her most hip-hugging jeans. She walked the cafeteria as if it were a fashion runway, parting the crowd as Moses did the Red Sea. All the boys dropped their jaws as they got a full view of her thong, which was color coordinated to match her purple baby tee and platform heels. If it weren't for her skin being so Wonder Bread White, I even might have bought that J-Ho could at least be part Latina. Ezekiel motioned for her to join him. He pulled her onstage and immediately they were in a lip-lock. Ezekiel cued the DJ and launched into "The Heavens Had a Plan" as a serenade to J-Ho.

> *Baby, I can't wait till that last school bell rings,*
> *When you and I can bounce from these walls, do our*
> > *thing.*
> *Not that I don't mind sneakin' kisses in the hallway,*
> *Whisper fantasies of you that I been thinkin' 'bout all*
> > *day.*
> *Tell by your smile that you been thinkin' 'bout me too,*
> *Tell me what you want, girl, I'm the man that can bring*
> > *you,*

The flowers, the rings and the love you deserve,
Ain't nobody but you can inspire these words.

My highest high, my lowest low, you ride or die by my
   side.
You shine so bright, color my world so I ain't no longer
   blinded.
Conquer the world, just be my girl, and then with you
   I'll divide it.

My highest high, my lowest low, you ride or die by my
   side.
You shine so bright, color my world, so I ain't no longer
   blinded.
Baby, the heavens had a plan when our two worlds col-
   lided.

I must confess when we first met, wasn't your heart I
   was after,
You was just another girl that I could add to the chapter.
But when you flowed up on the mic it was my heart that
   you captured.
Caught me off guard, soft lips rhyme hard, it turned me
   on and enraptured.
Curves for days, skin tone don't fade, and sweet like
   sunshine laughter,

*Takes care of me like royalty and does whatever I ask
    her.*
*No competition for the crown cuz we both microphone
    masters.*

*My highest high, my lowest low, you ride or die by my
    side.*
*You shine so bright, color my world, so I ain't no longer
    blinded.*
*Conquer the world, just be my girl, and then with you
    I'll divide it.*

*My highest high, my lowest low, you ride or die by my
    side.*
*You shine so bright, color my world, so I ain't no longer
    blinded.*
*Baby, the heavens had a plan when our two worlds col-
    lided.*

The crowd hollered and cheered for the horny, sappy couple. Personally, I've seen EZ do better, but he's whipped
and even brothas can get a little sappy sometimes. There's
a small group of Eminem wannabes that were waving
their hands as they would join in the chorus. Ezekiel's
always clownin' them as they try so hard to be Black and
down with hip-hop. Kinda funny given that he dates one
of them. Folks are so up in his mix that EZ could've

dissed them and they still would have thought he was cool.

I could deal until EZ just kept rubbing up on Jessica. Surprisingly, she pulled away when he got too close. I was miserable watching him gas her over and over. Why did he have to love her? That should be me. Didn't all those weeks at camp mean anything to him? I couldn't take it. I had to jet.

Sadie Matthews, Ezekiel's little sister and Lauryn Hill look-alike, slid into the chair next to me. Up to this point, I had been able to avoid her since we have no classes together. She's so smart, I'm sure she's in all the advanced classes. Whereas me, I got all the remedial courses except for history. Knowing my history only makes me a stronger emcee. My father used to say, "You need to know where you came from in order to know where you're going."

Sadie just kept staring at me, and I never could understand why. Hearing that she's been talking about me today from Bethany, though, made me think she doesn't like me. Maybe EZ told her to be my friend. She probably felt sorry for me. Just 'cause we're both freshmen and have a little melanin doesn't mean we'll get along. Sadie's a geek; well, I used to be one too until I came to this privileged school. Still, I'm not as good of a student as Sadie, especially now with all the craziness in my house with my dad leaving my mom. I just can't get motivated.

"Do you mind if I sit here? I just can't participate in another lovefest for my brother," said Sadie. "And can Jessica be more hooched out? Can a girl please represent by doing more than standing there all mute. I like it when girls are natural and confident."

I thought everyone loved EZ. I was really shocked by Sadie's reaction to him. Aren't younger sisters suppose to worship their older brothers? And I don't wear makeup, my skin is a little scarred from breakouts and my confidence sucks at the moment. Sadie is one of those Bayview/Hunter's Point girls who don't put up with anything. I was surprised that she could think for herself after seeing her kissing up to her trigonometry teacher in the hallway. Most freshmen are in algebra or maybe geometry, but trig?

"Nah, I'm just sittin' here by myself enjoying the hooch factor," I said.

"She bugs you too?" said Sadie.

"I just think it's easier for a pretty girl."

"So you must have it real easy." Sadie looked at me with the sweetest smile, which made me feel uncomfortable for some stupid reason.

"I'm not pretty. I've always been smart, at least until I came here. Now, I can't seem to bust higher than C's in any of my classes," I said.

"You're pretty, just not by White girl standards. It's your toughness that scares people away."

"Sadie, now you sound like your brother. What's he been saying?"

"He thought we could really kick it and be friends. He claims you're a tight emcee. That's yet to be determined until I see what you got. I'm an emcee too, but my folks wish I would give it up and just sing in the church choir."

I wished Ezekiel was the one calling me pretty and fine. Sadie does seem pretty cool. I kind of liked feeling sorry for myself, but she's so positive. I guess that's good that he thought about me. I wanted to be open, but given everything going on in my life right now it's hard to trust. Which isn't easy knowing that she talks to Bethany and Evita, my two least favorite people after J-Ho and Rio.

I'm curious to see if Sadie's raps are any good. Maybe if we became friends, I could see Ezekiel more often. It's not like I couldn't use a friend with Liza not being around and all. She and I were like the "dynamic duo" since elementary. We just understood each other. People never knew what Liza or I was. We always got asked, "What are you?" Since Liza is Filipina and White and on the fair side, in many ways she understood my issue with being a Black Latina. When people thought Asian or Latina, they didn't picture either of us. We stood up for each other and never tried to put the other in a box. We used to joke about how none of the families on television look like ours.

It must be harder for Liza being raised by a White

mother since her father died. Who does she turn to to learn about her Filipina side? She has brothers, but they're older and absorbed in their own lives. I used to love going to her house, it was always loud and lively. Liza's brothers were always doing b-boy moves in the kitchen. Someone was always fighting and they always had friends in their house. Their poor mother was always working, trying to feed five mouths. You would think that with Liza being the only girl, she would be spoiled, but life in the North Beach projects was usually about survival. If you came home, and there was no food, you didn't eat. I might not get expensive gifts or everything I wanted for Christmas, but at least I had my own room. Liza had to share a double bed with her mother and her four brothers lived in the living room.

Then Sadie fired away with her questions again. "Are you trying out for this talent show?"

"I might," I said, surprised she would ask me so soon.

"My best friend is a DJ. But we haven't been talking much lately. It's hard to meet anyone real at this school, so I've been thinking about forming my own crew."

"Yeah. I understand, I haven't seen my girl Liza much either."

"So, let's make it happen. How about you and Liza meeting up with us at my house after school tomorrow and showing us what you got?" said Sadie. "We'll make it a slumber party, so bring your clothes."

Sadie waited for my reaction. I was just a little

weirded out about spending the night at EZ's house. I was trying to stall so as to not seem too eager. I didn't really want to share the stage with two other girls I hardly knew. But I needed a crew and didn't really have any friends. At least Sadie seemed for real and not like some fake poser.

"I guess I could be down with you, once I see what you got," I said.

The crowd began to roar as EZ and J-Ho finished their performance. I turned away from Sadie long enough to see EZ give her a long juicy kiss. I wanted to puke. Then he patted her on the butt and got the other dudes in the crowd way too excited. I looked to Sadie and we both rolled our eyes.

"I hate PDA," I said.

"I'm with you. 'Sides, I've seen cuter."

"What?"

"I just mean she ain't all that."

"Oh," I said, now knowing why Sadie needs someone to write lyrics for her because she be mixing up her words all the time. Maybe she's just awkward socially. The bell rang and Sadie rushed off to class along with everyone else.

"See you later," said Sadie.

"Cool." I waved good-bye to Sadie and walked off toward Spanish class and who crashes into me? J-Ho, and we both dropped our book bags. I began to get pumped as she looked at me and smiled. This is my chance to rip her a new one and no one could blame me, right? I know she did it on purpose. Who gives a fuck that her five-foot-ten frame looming over my five-foot-two frame makes us look like David and Goliath.

"Sorry," she said, with her thin-lipped smirk.

I opened my mouth and said, "It's cool."

Idiota! I said to myself. How could I blow my chance to finally beat on the girl I hate most in the world, next to Bethany Doll? She did take away the love of my life. I reached down to pick up my bag, which was tangled on the buckle of her platform sandals. Perfect opportunity to make her lose her balance. Then I'd be the one saying, *"Hasta la victoria siempre!"* Like the true barrio warrior that my father has tried to make me. Instead, I picked up her bag and handed it to her.

"Thanks," she said. "Hey, aren't you Ezekiel's play sister from hip-hop camp?"

Oh, no she didn't go there! His sister? Do friends hang out every night until two in the morning? I don't think so. We hung out 24-7 during the summer. It was about to be on, but not before EZ came over to walk the ho to class. I attempted to rush toward my class.

"Hey, little sistah, where you been hiding?" he said, looking at me but putting his arm around J-Ho.

He didn't even give me his customary hug and kiss on the cheek. His six-foot-two frame looked perfect next to hers. How many times do I have to tell him, I'm not his "sis-tah." Like my day hadn't been bad enough, he then kisses her on the cheek. Disgusting!

"Just tryin' to survive the everyday struggle." I said.

I stuffed my feelings inside, so they couldn't come out. I have such a hard time getting mad at EZ. Now I know why my moms always took my father back. She loved him. I always thought she was mad stupid, but love has a way of doing crazy things to even strong-willed people. The closer someone gets to me, the harder it is for me to stand up for myself.

"Well, I really miss our battles," he said, making me melt.

Then he turned to J-Ho, ignoring me as she ran her fingers through his dreads. Gross. She touched his hair with a certain distance and intrigue. It made me sick.

"You got Jessica, practice with her. Why you checkin' for me now?"

EZ kissed her hand and then responded, "What?"

J-Ho then broke their couple moment. "Yeah, why don't you battle me? I'm a good emcee."

He nuzzled closer to her. " 'Cause I like to love you, not fight with you, boo."

J-Ho broke away from him. "We'll talk after school." She raced off to class without even a kiss on his cheek, leaving him and me alone in the cafeteria. Finally, an alone moment. EZ stood there looking sad, not even aware of me.

"Hey, I'm going to put my own crew together and try out for this talent show," I said.

"Cool," he said, his eyes following J-Ho as she left. He finally looked at me. "Why did you have to make her leave? You always gotta start something. Good luck in the talent show, Mariposa. Jessica is going to give you a run for your money."

"Obviously she's giving you a run for yours, *qué no*?"

Ezekiel rolled his eyes at me. "You wouldn't know love if it stared you in the face."

"How would you know? You're too busy chasing that White girl to notice anything else."

Ezekiel stepped toward me, looked into my eyes and said nothing. Then he bounced, leaving me alone in the big cold cafeteria. I knew I went too far, but I had to tell my truth. I felt like he was changing over J-Ho. Last summer every word out of his mouth was about loving his Nubian queens. I sucked the tears in before they could rush down my face. I leaned against the wall in the cafeteria and closed my eyes. I wanted to die. Nothing was worse than having EZ hate me.

CHAPTER 3

LATINA ENUF

I opened the door to class, knowing I was late and hoping that Liza had saved me a seat as she always sits close to the door. I had to put myself back together before dealing with my least favorite class, *Spanish*. I took a deep breath and sported my shades. I wanted to cut class but knew that would make my grade worse. Shit. Liza didn't save me a seat. I should have voted for the assigned seating option at the beginning of the semester when Señora Rivera gave the class a choice. It would have saved me from being humiliated by my only and supposed best friend at Stanford High School. I just sucked my teeth at Liza and searched for another seat. She didn't even notice because she was writing notes back and forth between her and her freaky boyfriend Rio.

"Good lookin' out, homie," I whispered under my breathe to Liza as I spotted another seat across the room.

When class has begun there's usually only one seat left and it's in front of Bethany and that sell-out Evita. I quietly made my way past Señora Rivera as she conjugated the verb *comer* into the imperfect tense on the board. She finished and glared at me for disturbing her lecture with my entrance. "Ms. Colón, maybe you can help me conjugate the verb *comer* in the future perfect tense."

She didn't even let me take a seat. That woman is always out to get me. I did my homework last night, but for the life of me I could only remember the present tense. "Umm, I can't remember."

I took my seat as everyone laughed. Even Liza looked away from Rio long enough to join in on the laughter, which made me feel even more stupid. It's not like Rio was the class genius. He hung out with all those iceheads. They do all kinds of crystal meth in the pit near the football field. I'm surprised he has enough brain cells to remember his class schedule.

Liza and I haven't been the same since she got with Rio this past summer. She seems more interested in hanging out with her capital L loser boyfriend than looking out for her homegirl. At first, I thought she was just out to prove she could get a guy, that somehow having a boyfriend made her more feminine and less of a tomboy. But after lunch today, I know she's just hooked on the *pendejo*. Their relationship reminds of me how flies are attracted to shit.

"Mariposa, you Hispanics who were born here never speak Spanish well. In my class you are going to learn to speak properly," said Señora Rivera.

Then Bethany Doll raised her hand and conjugated the verb: "*Habré comido, habrás comido, habrá comido, habremos comido* and *habran comido.*"

"*Bueno,*" said Señora Rivera, praising that brown-noser.

"Would you like the formal *vosotros* conjugation, as they use in Spain, too, Señora?" asked Bethany.

"Of course," said Señora Rivera.

"*Habréis comido,*" said Bethany.

What a suck-up! She then looked at Evita and they all laughed mockingly at me. How's a blonde-haired, blue-eyed White girl gonna speak better Spanish than me? Plus, I gotta take Spanish from a Spaniard who thinks all people outside of Spain butcher the language.

"Okay, that's enough laughing," said Señora Rivera, then she passed out our vocabulary list for tomorrow's quiz. "I need to run to the office, Bethany is in charge till I return."

Señora Rivera is not my favorite person. But at least when she's around the class has to maintain a certain amount of decorum. As she left, I became even more nervous about what was to come. Then it happened. Evita opened her mouth. "You're not really Hispanic if you don't speak Spanish." I ignored her comment while I pretended to be studying my vocabulary sheet.

Bethany had to open her mouth. "Is one of your parents African-American, 'cause you don't look like any Mexican person I know."

"I'm not Mexican. I'm not even 'his-panic.' I'm Puerto Rican. We're mixed with African, Spanish and Indian. I just happen to be more on the Black side," I said. "And what does my being Black have to do with me getting the wrong answer? I'm sick of people questioning it. Yet everywhere I turn the only Latinas represented on television or in the magazines look more White than Black. Even my mom has lighter skin and the kind of hair that she doesn't have to spend hours blow-drying straight."

"J. Lo's Puerto Rican and she looks different than you, and Evita speaks good Spanish," said Bethany.

"I'm not Puerto Rican," Evita said, like it was a curse. "I'm Nicaraguan."

Okay, now I really want to punch that smirk off her face. "Look, Miss Paris Hilton wannabe," I said to Bethany. "J. Lo's Puerto Rican when it's convenient. Her hair is really curly. She just has enough dough to pay a hairdresser to hook her up. You and your ducklings dress alike, walk alike, talk alike and look alike. But no one questions whether you're White, do they?"

Then Oscar, the only Chinese boy in Rio's posse, yells

out, "She sure has a J. Lo booty. I'd like to get a piece of that ass." I wasn't flattered by his attention, but I was happy to switch the subject. I was sick of playing teacher to a bunch of ignorant *blanquitos*. Or in Evita's case, coconuts: brown on the outside, white on the inside. Now the class was making fun of my *culito*, which is fine with me because it's the one thing lately that doesn't make me insecure.

"Sounds like you're just all mixed up," said Evita.

I rolled my eyes like I was about to undergo an exorcism. "You and I both know that the only reason why that 90210 wannabe Bethany is nice to you is so she can get an A in Spanish class. Well, when summer comes, don't come crying to me 'cause she dumped your butt."

Evita and Bethany gasped with shock, then shut up. A victory for me after such a horrible day! A part of me hated having to fight with Evita. If this was my barrio, we would have had each other's back. Here, street rules didn't apply.

Everyone laughed at Evita as she slumped down in her seat. I swear, I thought before she turned around her eyes would burn a stake through my chest.

"Mariposa has jokes," said Oscar, pointing at me as Señora Rivera reentered the room.

"All right, that will be enough. Class was going fine until you entered tardy and disrupted everyone's learning, Ms. Colón," said Señora Rivera. "I heard your voice all the way down the hall. You can stay after school to make up the time you missed."

"I gotta practice for the talent show auditions." Of course, I didn't really have practice. I just wanted to get as far from school as possible.

"You aren't going to be in any talent show if you fail my class."

Evita and Bethany sat there chuckling to themselves as Señora Rivera continued on with her lesson. I hated this school. All I could think about was why my parents never taught me Spanish. This class should be an easy A for me. Instead I gotta listen to everyone speaking better Spanish than me. And Ms. Evita trying to act like she's more Latina 'cause she can conjugate a stupid verb. I understand Spanish, just not the kind we're learning in this class. My words are more like Spanglish—a mix of Spanish and English. Why isn't there a class for that? We could call it Spanglish 101.

I'm tired of the fact that the only things these kids know about being Puerto Rican comes from television, magazines or music. And since I live in California, they think all Latinos are Mexican. I guess I have my own stereotypes to check, 'cause they really can hurt. Oscar in his own way had my back and I continue to call him a geeky Chinese kid. I guess that's not cool; it's still hurtful and prejudiced.

CHAPTER 4

BONDING WITH SOUL SIREN

After school, I reported to the library to serve out detention for my supposed outburst in Señora Rivera's class. Lucky for me, I attend a college preparatory school where detention is unsupervised. All you have to do is sign in and sign out.

Given that my day was so wonderful, I decided to work on my lyrics for the talent show. I put my pen to the paper and all I could write was "I Love EZ" over and over again. I surfed the Internet and discovered gurl.com, which has become one of my favorite websites next to verbalisms.com, an online magazine for women in hip-hop. There was this article about teenagers and depression. It said that a growing number of Latinas are beginning to suffer from depression. Never really saw myself as the depressed type, until lately. According to gurl.com I suffer from all the warning signs: lack of social acceptance, a broken family, loss of appetite, oversleeping, academic failure and rejected in love. According to them, I'm the perfect candidate for suicide, drug addiction and alcoholism.

Speaking of addict, Rio, who never goes to school, is in the library and I know he doesn't have detention. He's shaking hands with Eddie Heinrich, whose father owns Heinrich Catsup. Normally Eddie wouldn't be seen with the likes of Rio, but Eddie is known around school for inheriting his father's entrepreneurial skills. Like father like son, Dad exploits laborers in Mexico and Eddie keeps the druggies supplied.

After seeing the transaction go down between Eddie and Rio, I started to feel like maybe my life wasn't so horrible after all. I did wonder where Liza was though, and was both surprised and relieved that she wasn't with Rio.

I heard some giggling behind me. Evita and Bethany were hiding out in the back and I swear I saw Evita's hand brush against Bethany's in a way you only do when you want to get with someone. First I was shocked and then I was grossed out. Two girls is just weird. Then it made sense to me why they were friends. No one would ever think either of them was gay. What a perfect cover.

Sadie entered the library and headed toward Evita. She immediately hugged her, and for the first time ever I saw Evita smile. I just can't see Sadie and Evita being friends. Sadie is so grounded and aware of herself. I guess all leaders need someone to follow them. Being followed seems to be a common thing for the Matthews family. Even Bethany was trying to chat up Sadie. But Sadie said her two cents and headed toward me.

"Hey you, what you doing here?"

"Serving out detention," I said quickly, trying to hide my childish love notes to her brother.

"Sounds like fun. I guess I'm gonna have to keep you out of trouble," said Sadie, trying to peep what I was doing.

Then I got defensive. "I don't need anyone's help."

"Cool. Just trying to create conversation, help pass the time," said Sadie.

From the corner of my eye, I could see Evita staring at me like she was jealous or something. "I'm sorry it's just, you know, Evita and Bethany, and they're part of the reason that I'm sitting here."

"First, I don't like Bethany," said Sadie. "I only deal with her to keep the peace between Evita and me. Our parents are friends, since Evita's dad is the janitor of the same school where my mother is the principal. The only place where she can spend time is either on the school premises or at my house."

"No offense, but Evita's fake," I said. Trying not to care, I noticed it was 4:30 P.M. so I began to gather my books and stuff them into my backpack.

"Just confused and hurt. Us not being friends is really my fault. I kinda hurt her feelings," Sadie said.

I didn't understand how Sadie could ever do anything to hurt that made-of-steel Evita. "What, by telling her about herself?"

"Not exactly. I really don't want to talk about it right now," said Sadie, attempting to avoid my questions. "You wanna go check out Amoeba Records with me on Haight Street?"

"That's like one of my favorite places to go."

"Mine too," she said.

"Last time I was there I discovered Mystic, this amazing emcee from Oaktown."

"I've never heard of her," said Sadie.

"I would burn you a copy, but you gotta support the sistah."

"I did get this great old school DVD on the history of hip-hop. It was fresh, but I just wish there was more females represented," said Sadie.

"That's why we gotta exercise our chops and get good."

It felt so good to have a real conversation about something I loved besides EZ. Just talking with Sadie started to make me feel lighter and free. All those thoughts about not trusting her because she was friends with Evita just disappeared. I was just happy to have a friend.

I signed out of detention with Sadie eagerly behind

me. "Don't think just because you got me all excited about Amoeba that you're off the hook from telling me what happened between you and Evita."

For the first time since we spoke the other day, Sadie didn't have a response or a question. She just smiled. I knew though that whatever she was keeping from me had to be good. "Cat got your tongue? Ms. One Thousand Questions doesn't have an answer?"

"Shut up," said Sadie. Then she reached inside her pocket and pulled out a Minnie Mouse Pez dispenser and one by one with great precision she inserted a package of grape candies. "Want one?"

"No, I only like the orange ones," I said, waiting for at least one of the tiny candies to fall to the ground, but none did. I waited for her to pull out a package of orange ones, but she didn't.

"I love the orange ones too, but EZ has been hoarding all those since this summer. Dudes always be thinking about themselves. And Pez is hard to come by; my mother buys them for us by the case at Costco."

I just smiled because I knew that EZ hated the orange ones. It gave me hope that maybe he took all the orange ones for me. Sounds crazy, but it made a really bad day hella bright.

CHAPTER 5

LOVE THY SELF

It was winter in San Francisco and it had been raining all week. Some of the rain had managed to leak past the crumbling wood around the windowsill, puddling in its corners. The rain dripped over my poster of Mystic, making her look as if she were crying. Or maybe it was just my heart. It had been a week since Sadie and I had gone to Amoeba Records. But we had been speaking on the phone every day and bonding over our deepest secrets.

I sat on the end of my twin bed, which I've had since the third grade, scratching the pills on Gizmo, the blanket I've had since I was a baby. I would die if anyone knew about Gizmo. God knows how many times my mother has tried to hide her from me, saying I was too old for her. Papi always managed to get her back for me, recovering her from the trash. My mother would wash Gizmo, claiming the need to keep her clean, but for some reason she kept getting smaller and smaller. I soon discovered that each time she washed her she would cut her, hoping that eventually she would disappear. So now, every morning when I wake up I wrap Gizmo in a shirt and hide her in the back of my closet before I leave for school.

What time was it? I rubbed the sleep from my eyes and looked at my clock. It was only 7:00 P.M. I moved to my desk, which was now too short for even my five-foot-two frame, to finish my list. I stopped rubbing my eyes and frowned at the piece of paper in front of me, trying to ignore the sheets of rain cascading against the window. The apartment felt damp and cold. I cradled Gizmo on my lap, rubbing her occasionally for comfort.

The ten things I must do to win Ezekiel's love by Mariposa Colón. Carefully, I underlined it. Underneath, in my best handwriting, my list read:

1. Become the best female rapper ever. (Even I can dream.)
2. Win the school talent show competition.
3. Become friends with Sadie and her homegirl so I can see Ezekiel.
4. Cast a spell on Ezekiel.

5. Buy some sexy outfits that will catch his eye. (No, I'm not becoming a hoochie.)
6. Become more social at school.
7. Stop sweatin' Ezekiel, and act like I've moved on.
8. Spend time with EZ one on one.

I stopped and began to chew on my nails, really doubting that this plan would ever work. It felt like too much work. Talking to Sadie today made me think about not being so self-conscious. After all, the biggest thing J-Ho had going for her was her self-confidence. My mom was the perfect example. When I was younger, she always looked so sexy, and now her mind seems heavy and her eyes are full of bags. Mom didn't get ugly. She just lost herself. I don't ever want to feel like my life is over. I don't want to be alone and sad. What if I follow my dreams and in the end I still lose EZ?

When I was younger I lived my life according to how Papi thought I should believe. Being a former Young Lord, Papi had certain radical beliefs about life that were different from Mami's. The Young Lords were this 1960s radical Puerto Rican group that started in Chicago and moved to New York, modeling themselves after the Black Panthers that started in Oakland, California.

I was only a year old when we moved from New York to San Francisco so my father could get a better job working for my godfather as a mechanic in his new shop. We still barely made any money, so he took a second job driving a taxi. Leaving his family and friends from New York was difficult for Papi, but he did it because he loved Mami and would do anything to make her happy. Perhaps Papi got tired of feeling like second best and he just gave up one day.

It's hard for me to think of Papi being anything but confident. I came running home from school in second grade crying to my father, saying, "They said I wasn't Mexican, Papi, that I'm Black."

Papi took me in his arms, running his calloused hands through my curly hair. "See this beautiful hair? Only Puerto Rican girls have hair like this, and carmel skin that glows under the sunlight. *Nenita,* you're special."

"I don't care about being special. I want to be Mexican, not Black," I said, crossing my arms and pouting.

I didn't realize what I was saying then, but I swear I saw smoke come out of my father's ears. "You don't need those Mexican kids, you're a *Boricua.* You come from a proud and brave people."

"Sounds like a barracuda fish," I said.

Papi then bent down to his knees. "Next time they tease you about being 'too Black,' you say, *'Despierta Boricua, defiende la tuya.'* Then look at them and tell them to wake up Aztlán, go defend your own." Then he raised his fist not to scare me, but to show his defiance, like a real revolutionary.

I get it now, Papi was teaching me to be proud and that those kids didn't know enough about their own history to be teasing me about mine. For months, I went through the hallways yelling what Papi told me. In the end it finally got me in trouble as some of the Mexican parents didn't appreciate all that Chicano talk about Aztlán.

When most kids were going to church on Sunday, we were participating in protests to free Mumia Abu-Jamal or the Puerto Rican Political Prisoners. Papi stopped for a while, but the more Mami drank the more he used his politics like a religion. Papi didn't care about money, he just cared about the struggle. Mami wanted to be a dancer and settled for Papi. They just argued about money and how he cared more about his stupid movement than my mother. They both lived someone else's dream without ever figuring out what made each of them happy.

I've gone from being a budding revolutionary to a love-struck fool who makes lists about catching a guy who loves someone else. My stomach started to tighten. I never wanted to be too scared to follow my dreams. I started writing again.

9. Figure out what makes me happy.
10.

I put my arms on the desk and watched outside as the thunder clapped harder, then rumbled back into oblivion. I wondered if my mother ever really loved him as much as he loved her. Mami never has been as affection-ate as Papi. Maybe his new girlfriend makes him feel loved. But then Papi just up and left and hasn't even called me. Something has to be wrong with him too. How can any father just leave the woman he supposedly loved and then punish his child by not even calling? He's selfish. I hate him right now, a feeling I never thought I would feel toward him.

I frowned and thought about how stupid people can be sometimes. Especially fathers. He would always ask, "How much does your Papi love you?"

"Infinity," I said.

"Half right. Infinity times infinity," said Papi. Then he would take his fingers and make a sideways number eight across his heart. And I would just smile feeling I was the luckiest little girl in the world to have so much love.

"Mariposa, *comida*," said my mother in her Puerto Rican accent.

"I'll be there in a second, Mami."

I read through my list again. Number ten defeated me. I decided to keep the slot open in case another idea came to me later. My list wasn't quite right. There were things—important things—that I had left out. I was sure of it.

I could hear my mother's footsteps coming down the hall. Soon she would ask me to join her for dinner and my moment of peace would be ruined by her drunken self-pity.

My mother peeked in through the door. "You got lots of homework?"

I gazed at my mother in shock. It's probably the first time in months that she has asked me how I am. Every day she comes home to fix dinner, locks herself in her room and drinks herself to sleep with wine. When she did talk, it was usually about how sad she is over my father leaving us. I usually pretended not to be interested. It's not like I don't have my own problems.

"I'm just brainstorming ideas for a paper I'm writing."

"What's it about?" she asked.

I was really weirded out. I wondered what she wanted. Even when Papi lived with us, Mami was always in her own world. I would come home from school. She would cook and then lock herself in her room watching her *novelas*. Since she never spent time with me, I thought she never really wanted to have me. Papi told me she loved me, but giving up dance broke her heart. He didn't make enough money working his two jobs, so she had to start cleaning houses to help pay the bills. She never complained about it, but she did tune out and went into her own world where no one could touch her. I wished she would talk to me about her childhood and growing up in Puerto Rico again, but she acted like she had no life before Papi and me.

"I'm writing an essay about what I want to be when I grow up," I said.

"What do you want to be?"

"I'd like to be a Latina rapper. There's only about three or four of us that have made it. I wanna inspire people with my flow."

"What's 'flow'?"

"The way I say my music. I'll demonstrate. I have this song I've been working on, but I've only been able to finish a part of it."

Mami sat next to me on my bed. I quickly turned over my paper. I was waiting for her to say something about how bad hip-hop is and how I will never become a rapper. "I'm waiting, go."

"Remember, it's rough," I said, finally gathering the courage to recite my unfinished song. "I kind of got inspired by Katrina with this one." Then as my Mami watched, I performed, adding a little human beat-box effect.

The harsh reality of life
watch how it unfolds,
Mother Nature you just can't control.
Separated by the system,
made us into victims,
conquered by design
wish my people could elevate their mind.

Realized that the gov't don't care about poor people,
separated by class,
'cuz we are not equal.

Beggin' for food and water,
polluting the air,
children separated,
'cuz their parents not there.

Ended up with nothing,
that's why I stand for something.
I'm definitely not running,
'cuz Bush and them is not coming.
Flood waters raging,
it's just freakin' amazing.

Who's a survivor,
'cuz I'm not a looter.
Who got the guns and the
hired sharpshooters?
We gotta get to higher ground,
elevate my people with the sound
On the microphone.

You know how I get down,
want more out of life,
but Black people
we always gotta fight.
Put my fist in the air
because this world is not fair.

Then I finished and Mami just stood there and watched, crying. "I know it's rough, but I was hoping it wasn't *that* bad," I said.

Mami reached her arms out and pulled me toward her. "It was beautiful, you just reminded me of your father with your fist in the air." It felt good to be seeing her crying when she wasn't drunk.

It was in that moment that I realized that my mother did love my father and some hard place in me was softened by her crying. I was more afraid that she wouldn't get it with all the slang I used in the song. Sometimes I felt it was hard to communicate with her because my Spanish was so bad. Being close to Papi was a bit easier, seeing that he was raised in New York and spoke both equally well. But my mother convinced my father to not speak Spanish to me. She didn't want me to struggle like she did by speaking with an accent.

Don't get me wrong, my mother spoke good English, she just pretended not to when it was convenient. Like when I was in fifth grade and needed to put a family tree together. She refused to talk about her family and just kept pretending that she didn't understand the assignment.

Mami stopped crying. "Hip-hop is like poetry. When I was a girl in Puerto Rico I had this boyfriend that would flow to me, like Run-DMC," she said.

"Mom, how do you know who Run-DMC is?"

"*Mira*, your dad's fifty-eight, he's the *viejo*. I'm only forty."

"They had hip-hop in Puerto Rico?"

"Everywhere *la gente* were always going back and forth between New York and Puerto Rico. My boyfriend was from the South Bronx and he would teach me about things there," she said.

It was so weird to think that my mother was alive when hip-hop started. She always seemed so ancient to me. Not the way she looked, just the way she acted.

"Were you in love with him, Mami?"

"*Sí*, he was as sweet as *azúcar*," said Mami. "Umm, was he sweet." My mom started cooling herself off with her hand and then began to laugh uncontrollably. I joined her, surprised that I was able to share something so personal with her.

"On Fridays, I use to get all fancy and walk around the plaza with him in Ponce," she said. "All the girls liked him, but he had eyes for me *solamente*. He made me feel special and beautiful. I would paint pictures for him and he would write the words to what they mean."

"Sounds like you really liked each other."

"I was so happy. So young and full of dreams."

"What did your parents think of him, Mami?"

The laughter stopped. Mami became teary-eyed again and I just wanted her to share with me why. She clammed up and when that happened it was like breaking through a brick wall. All I could do was put my arm around her and comfort her as she sobbed. I could've kicked myself for putting my foot in my mouth. I should have left well enough alone.

My mom stopped crying, wiped her eyes and then looked at me. "I got a call from your school today."

I looked toward the ceiling. "And?"

"Señora Rivera called and said you were supposed to stay after school to make up the time you were late for class. She said you have a D in her class. How could you have a D in Spanish when you're Puerto Rican?"

"It's not like we ever spoke Spanish at home."

"Spanish is a lot easier than English. How about if I help you?"

"You're always working and I didn't want to bother you."

"*Pero, mija,* I love you and I want you to do well."

"You do?" I asked. I couldn't remember the last time she said those words to me.

"*Sí,* Mariposa. You are the best thing I've ever done."

"Really?" Wow, it was hard for me to believe that she really felt that way. How could I be the best thing she'd ever done when I'm not much of anything yet? I sucked in the tears, as my mom did enough crying for both of us in one night. Then she hugged me real quick, but it felt good. I can't remember the last time she hugged me before tonight. My father was always the affectionate one.

"Mami, I miss him but just can't forgive him for leaving us for that woman. I really hate her."

"Me too," she said.

"Just promise me one thing."

"What?"

"That you'll stop drinking 'cause I couldn't bear to lose you both."

"Cross *mí corazón*," she said making the sign of the cross. "Now, let's eat and then we'll work on your Spanish."

The doorbell rang. "I'll get it, Mami." I rushed to the door like a little girl anticipating that her father would walk through the door after a long day at work.

Our apartment is small. There's a living room at the front of the house. The next room is my parents', well, now Mami's, so you have to walk through it to get to the living room and back through it again to get to my room. Then there's the kitchen and the bathroom, which falls off of my room like the bottom of an L. Sliding wood doors separate Mami's room from the living room, where there are so many plants in the two windows that when the doors are open, it looked as though you've walked into a jungle. I watered them and kept them growing now that my Papi was gone. Mami pushed them aside to look out onto our noisy block or at her photo of the Last Supper. There's a door separating my and Mami's rooms and we always kept it closed since she often wanted to be alone.

I opened the door to find Liza. "What are you doing here?"

"We got a talent show to prepare for," she said. She threw her bag filled with clothes on the couch, which usually meant she planned on staying overnight.

"Shouldn't you be with Rio?" I said, hoping that would scare her away. After Spanish class I was prepared to finally write off our friendship. I was tired of the way she loses herself in her boyfriends and forgets that anyone else exists.

She didn't leave, she just stood there smiling. I could have forgiven her for being absent from my life lately, but not having my back in Spanish class and ignoring me in the cafeteria: that wasn't cool.

"He's out with his friends. And we haven't had time to chill," said Liza.

I rolled my eyes at her, not really caring if she left or stayed. I walked away, leaving her alone at the door. In typical Liza fashion she invited herself into my house, dropped her duffel bag on my bed and followed me into the kitchen, where my mom had prepared my favorite meal, *arroz y gandules* and *pasteles*.

"Oh, hi Liza," my mom said, surprised to see her.

"Hi, Mrs. Colón," said Liza, sizing up our food with excitement.

"Are you spending the night?" asked Mom.

"Yeah, I forgot to tell you," I said.

"No worries, *mija*. You two can eat here and I'll make another plate and eat in my room."

For once I wanted my mom to be mad and kick her out. This was our night and I needed her. I wanted to be selfish and just think about myself.

Liza took a seat at the kitchen table, which only seats two people comfortably. When Dad left, my mom threw out anything that reminded her that he once lived with us, including the dining room table he built. It was a beautiful cherry wood and on each leg he had etched dancing palm trees so that my mom could have a piece of Puerto Rico in our house. He even built four chairs, a special one for each of us and an extra one for a guest. I can't remember how many times Papi and I played cards or he helped me with my homework while sitting at that table. I was really sad to see it go.

"Sorry, Mami, can I take a rain check?"

She leaned over and kissed me. "Sure, tomorrow." Then my mom made herself a plate and left, but not before she poured herself a glass of cheap Chablis that came in a box.

Clueless, Liza just sat at the table and started eating.

"Your mom sure can cook." She then took a sip of her ginger ale and burped.

"Gross, Liza."

She ignored me, and just kept eating. I looked at Liza, shocked by how clueless she was. Then I remembered that she had four brothers who treated her like one of the guys. Liza's oldest brother Abraham was the main parental figure, but he left for college a year ago. Her other brothers were just plain selfish and fended for themselves, which is probably why Liza is so skinny.

She's such a tomboy. I used to think she might be gay, but then she discovered boys and they became the center of her world. But it wasn't until Rio that she stopped really being a b-girl. She would come to my house and create moves to go with my beats. It was awesome! But now it was all about Rio. Personally, I think Rio got jealous of her talent, 'cause he couldn't bust a move to save his crankhead life.

Liza finished her food, left her plate on the table and started toward my room.

"Clean your plate first," I said.

"What?" She then looked at me and put the plate in the sink where it belonged. But she didn't wash it or even scrape it clean. She just left it there with food crusted all over it.

"Fine. Leave it there for the cockroaches. You're the one sleeping on the floor."

She picked up the plate and acted like she didn't know what to do with it. Like dudes do when they don't want to do something, hoping a woman will take over and do it for them. Not me.

"Now take the plate, scrape the food in the garbage, wash it with soap and put it on the dish rack. I'm not Puerto Rican Rella," I said.

Liza sucked her teeth, but did as instructed. Finally, progress. I am so happy to be an only child. How you gonna come to someone's house, leave your plate in the sink and not wash it? Some people have *no home training*.

"Hey, Mariposa, I'm sorry I was stank to you in the cafeteria and in Spanish class."

See, that's how Liza gets me every time. She gets me mad and then she just switches up. I gave her the evil eye.

"Seriously, I really miss hanging with you."

"Whatever."

"You're my only homegirl."

"Well, you're the only female I know that acts like a dude," I said.

"C'mon, I'll give you a card reading. I know you love 'em," she said.

And she's right, I do like that otherworldly stuff. I front like I don't, but I am a little superstitious. What Latino isn't?

"First, I gotta tell you something I've been dying to share."

Liza perked up now that she was almost out of the doghouse. "What?"

"When I went to detention last week, I saw Evita and Bethany holding hands in the library."

"So, maybe they were supporting each other. That doesn't mean anything."

"No, they were touching each other like you do when you have a boyfriend," I said, sure that I was right.

"C'mon, Mari, you're reading into it. We all know how you love those two? 'Sides, so what if they are a couple, let it be."

My reaction was instant. "Well, don't you think it's kinda gross?"

"No." Liza gave me a bewildered stare. "You never wanted to, like, do it with a girl?"

"No. I guess I'm part of the ten percent."

"What?"

"I was reading on gurl.com that some test happened where they figured out that ten percent of the population is totally straight, ten percent is totally gay and the other eighty percent are bisexual."

"Gay or straight?" teased Liza.

"Straight, of course!" Then I thought about what I had just said, and wondered if I could really be somewhere in the middle. I did have my first kiss with a girl in third grade. Then we got busted by the principal and they made such a big deal about it, I had erased it from my memory until this very moment.

"I could get with a girl if she was cute," Liza said.

"Yeah, I'm sure you'll sleep with enough people in high school for the both of us."

"Oh, so now I'm a ho?" said Liza, looking surprised by my proclamation.

"I didn't say that, you're just easy."

Liza sighed. "Well if I'm easy, you're the Virgin Mary."

Then we just laughed. Liza took my punches because she knew she had them coming.

She then headed to the table, pulled out her deck and began shuffling. It looked like any other deck of cards with the exception that it was made in the Philippines, where her father was born and raised. Liza's dad was a bit of a gambler before he died and she always remembered him teaching her all kinds of card tricks. Supposedly, she looks a lot like him with lighter skin, but all her family photos were destroyed when we were in fifth grade and their apartment caught on fire. The only thing Liza saved from the fire were those cards and she created this game called Balikbayan Readings which, in Tagalog, means someone who is going back home. She believed that her readings are guided by her father's spirit who wanted nothing more than to return home to the Philippines a rich man so his family would never be hungry again. Ironically, he left his family hungry here.

I finally came around. "Okay." And I headed to the table to join Liza.

"You know I just want you and Rio to get along," said Liza. "I'm hoping that one of these weekends we can all go out to eat."

I made a face. "Why do I have to be there when you go on a date with him?"

"Because Rio is important to me."

"And?"

"And you're important to me. So I want my two best friends to come together."

"Can't we go to a movie? This way we don't have to talk too much," I said.

Liza smiled. "Your treat?"

"Maybe. If you learn to act right," I said. Then I sat on the edge of the couch and eyed Liza's cards. "How about that reading?"

"So what do you want to know," said Liza.

"I like a certain guy. Can you tell me if I have a chance?"

Liza then cleared a space on the table and rubbed her hands together. She separated the cards in two piles—one with only numbers and the other with only face cards.

"Okay, pick four cards from each pile and place them face down in two separate rows."

She then pulled out two toothpicks from behind her

ears, which she called her "tinkling sticks." "Now, let your fingers hop over and outside the sticks three times. Then pick a card from each pile without letting me capture your fingers with the sticks."

My question, of course, was will I ever have a chance with Ezekiel? Of course, Liza could never know. I picked one card from each pile. She turned them over—the five of hearts and the queen of hearts.

"The numbered cards are used to identify the probability of you getting what you want. The face cards are the end result," said Liza.

"So what do they mean?" I asked.

"Well, the five of hearts means you have a fifty percent chance of getting this guy. But the queen of hearts means that no matter what happens, his heart is in your hands."

"So, what can I do to make this happen," I said with honest curiosity.

"Pick another card from each pile."

I was surprised when I picked the ten of hearts and the ace of hearts. The probability of choosing four cards of the same suit is very slim. Liza just studied the cards. "Well, love is definitely on your mind. What I get from this is that your odds for love are high according to the ten card. But the ace tells me you must learn to love yourself first."

"What do you mean? Of course I love myself!"

"The ace means that you have to be alone and the heart means love; you figure it out."

"This is stupid. I can't believe I'm actually going along with this," I said.

Liza just looked me dead in the eyes. "Okay then, tell me ten things you love about yourself."

I looked her in the eyes and prepared to fire away. "Well, I love my *culito*."

"All right, that's one."

I kept trying to think of something, but for some reason nothing came.

"You're a dope emcee," said Liza.

"Yeah, I guess I'm all right."

"Now you give me one," she said.

Then I noticed this huge bruise around her wrist as she gathered the cards together.

"How'd you get that?" I asked.

"Oh, I was wrestling one of my brothers and he held me down too long."

"Which one?" I asked, not believing her.

Liza took a deep breath and quickly glanced around the room, then finally made eye contact with me. "Abraham."

"You sure?"

Liza winced and said, "I would tell you if anything was wrong," and then she pulled her sleeve back over her wrist.

I felt like the world's worst friend. Here I was feeling all hurt. Needing Liza back so I had someone to listen to my problems and I never asked her what was up with her. I knew something had to be going on that Liza wasn't ready to tell me or she was in denial. I remember when our math teacher in junior high used to make weird comments to Liza and she never spoke a word of it till he cornered her alone one day when she was working on the yearbook after school. Lucky for her, I decided to join her and ruined his plans. Liza never speaks until it's too late and she has nowhere else to turn. Then she's like an open book, tears and all. I just hoped things with Rio wouldn't get that bad.

"Are you okay?"

"Yeah, I'm fine," Liza mumbled. "I'm kind of tired, I'm gonna get ready for bed if you don't mind."

I directed her to the hallway closet and pointed to the towels. "My mom moved everything around since my dad left."

Liza disappeared into the bathroom. I decided to get ready for bed. I noticed my book and picked it up. Once again I found myself staring at the list. So, where was I? Yeah, number ten on my list. Determined to finish this list, I just stared, hoping it would reveal itself to me.

I started thinking about all these secrets I keep to myself that get in the way of anyone really getting close to me. Sometimes I'm just hard and that pushes people away. I end friendships before they can even start. Sadie was one of the first people that had broken through that wall. But she's like EZ, she doesn't take no for an answer. If I'm serious about EZ I need to learn to listen and be open to his side of things too. So, though number ten will be the most difficult, it may be the very thing that brings EZ and I together. In large letters I scrawled out number ten.

10. Be open.

CHAPTER 6

HIS STORY OR MINE

It rained again today, a warm, steady rain that turned the entire city gray. I sat in Mr. Leash's class watching it. There was something sad about the rain. My dad left my mom and me on a rainy day. The day he moved out it rained and rained. I turned back to my sketchbook, bored as Mr. Leash lectured. I wondered if I'd see Ezekiel at Sadie's house after school. I hadn't seen him all day. That's what the rain made me feel now as it slammed against the windowpane—that I should stop hoping. People always disappeared.

I decided to work on my lyrics since I was meeting up with Sadie and her crew after school to show them my skills. Eventually, the words just started to flow. I felt mad excited as I wrote in my sketchbook, hidden behind my history book.

"Mariposa, I know you're more interested in writing love notes, but if you listened you might find what I'm teaching you helpful on your next test. And just maybe if you study you can actually pass this test."

I just rolled my eyes and continued on with what I was doing. History is the one class I could pass in my sleep. My father was always quizzing me with questions like, "Who discovered America?"

"The Pilgrims?"

"No, the Native Americans." Then he would launch into this lecture about Native American rights, which then led to a discussion about slavery and the Middle Passage.

"I'd like all twenty-seven amendments memorized by—" Mr. Leash was saying.

"Excuse me."

The room changed. The air around me grew warm suddenly—and still.

"I've been transferred over from Ms. Boneparte's class. My name is Sadie."

I lifted my head slowly, afraid I had heard right. She was standing there—in front of the room—finally someone to chill with in class.

Mr. Leash frowned as he studied Sadie's program card. "This late into the semester, Ms. Matthews?"

"Yes, sir." Sadie took a quick look around the room. Her eyes flicked past me, then back again. She smiled.

"Well, take a seat then," Mr. Leash said. "Look on with someone. You can pick up a textbook from my office at the end of the day. Memorize all twenty-seven amendments by Monday. Are you familiar with the amendments?"

"Yes, sir." Sadie looked annoyed.

"Good then. Take a seat."

She looked around the room again and nodded hello to a couple of people before walking slowly up the aisle toward me.

"Can I sit next to you?"

I nodded. She had her hair pulled back in a ponytail today. When she sat down and smiled again, I smiled back. The smile felt shaky. Maybe I was trembling a little. Sadie just made me a little nervous. It's her intensity. She has these high expectations and I don't think I will ever measure up. I'm used to being the one that sets the standard in my friendships. With Sadie, I'm gonna have to learn to be a follower sometimes.

"Can I look on with you too?"

I nodded again, pressing my nails into my palms. My skin felt as though it would lift off.

"Can I have your book for keeps?"

I stared at her without saying anything, not sure what she was talking about. She grinned.

"I'm kidding."

"Oh." She has jokes. Cool.

"The right to privacy . . ." Mr. Leash was saying.

Sadie leaned over to look on with me. She smelled of freesias. I stared down at the page and inhaled.

"Why'd you get transferred out of the other class?" I whispered.

"I knew it already. Remedial history. School made a mistake."

"They do stuff like that all the time."

"Yeah, it just seems more common when it happens to me. What made them think I needed remedial anything? Nobody tested me. They just threw me in it then looked surprised when I knew it all. It makes you wonder—is it my hair?" she said and smiled.

"Or the melanin thing?" I said. "Well, I don't know how advanced this class is, all we keep learning about is these stupid amendments so we can grow up to be outstanding citizens that uphold the status quo."

"Well, there was no room in the honors class. And the other teacher didn't really like me," said Sadie.

We both noticed Mr. Leash staring at us. "Don't know if he'll be any better," I whispered.

We both laughed out loud. "I wonder if Lauryn Hill ever felt this bored when she was doing her bid at Columbia University, when she really wanted to be making her music," said Sadie.

"True that. But I didn't know she studied in South America," I said.

Sadie started to laugh and I really didn't think what I

said was all that funny. "You're too cute. Columbia University in New York City. Not the country."

I felt so embarrassed. I should've kept my mouth shut. I slid lower into my seat and just kept writing. I've never left California so how was I supposed to know? One time my mom even let me go to Oaktown with my then-best friend Nicole and her older sister Rochelle to see Missy Elliott. For me that was a big deal.

I guess Sadie felt bad because she said, "I only know because my dad grew up in Harlem, and he's always telling EZ and me that all his hard work would pay off if either of us got into Columbia."

I ignored her because I still felt stupid. What's so big about Columbia University? The biggest thing it has going for it in my opinion is that it's in New York and Lauryn Hill went there, but even she left.

Mr. Leash was eyeing us. I turned to a clean page in my sketchbook and wrote "Mariposa" across the top of it. Then my book—as well as the hidden sketchbook—fell onto the floor. Mr. Leash rushed to pick it up. I freaked out because I spent last night writing this song about EZ, instead of doing my homework. He read the title of my latest song aloud, "I Wanna Be Your Boo." Then he began to recite it to the class, which sounded retarded coming from someone with no flava.

You bring out the homegirl in me
The battle rhyme

Lose track of time
Kick it on the corner
Late night bus ride in me.

You bring out the straight-faced lie in me
The I can do it better than you in me
The laugh now cry later
Truth or dare in me.

You bring out the little girl laughing in me
The proud girl betta watch your step in me.
The sweet lips thick curves li'l mami in me
Bet my hips match the rhythm of yours in me
You bring out the tender side I can't show you in me.

You bring out the I wanna be your girl in me
The carve your initials in the tree trunk
Watch you when you ain't lookin'
Jasmine oil dabbed behind my ears
Memory of your mango juicy lips in me.
The hoping hoping never doubting they'll touch mine
     in me.
The hoping hoping never doubting myself in me.

The class just laughed. A few of the boys yelled out, "Mariposa is in love. How cute!"

Busting me out like that just wasn't cool. They don't

need to know my business. At that moment all I wanted
to do was leave the stupid school. But I was getting tired
of that uppity Mr. Leash making me feel like I couldn't
make it at this whack school. Maybe if he taught me
something I could relate to and showed a little respect, I'd
pay attention.

He then slammed both books on my desk. "Mariposa,
are you familiar with the Miranda Law?" he yelled in my
ear.

"Yes, sir. The right to remain silent," I said, looking
him straight in the face.

"Good, maybe you and Ms. Matthews can do that
right now."

The class laughed and Sadie smiled. She had a beautiful smile.

"Actually, back to amendments, I like the first one—
freedom of speech. Which I feel is often disrespected in
this classroom if we don't agree with your opinions," I
said.

Mr. Leash walked closer to me, but not before Sadie
blared out, "My personal favorite is the second one—the
right to bear arms, shall not be infringed."

The class really laughed at that one. The bell rang and
my classmates broke out, leaving Sadie and me with the
biggest smirks on our faces. We were quite proud of our-
selves for standing up to him.

"Get to your next class," he said.

I grabbed my books and bolted out the door. Next to seeing EZ on the bus the other day, I've never been so happy to have someone join me.

"Thanks for havin' my back," I said.

"Did you ever doubt I wouldn't?" said Sadie.

She made me feel so special. I began to believe that she and I were going to become good friends. I hadn't felt that sure about any friend since Nicole. She and I were girls from second grade till she moved away in the middle of junior high. I was devastated, because I just don't get close to people that easily. I'm not good at the casual chitchat thing.

"I guess I've just gotten used to goin' it alone," I said.

"My pleasure. Soul Siren at your service. Now, let's head over to my house so we can hear you kick some of those sappy lyrics I heard in class. I just want to know one thing."

My face turned red. Sadie had read me like a book. Please don't ask me if those lyrics were for Ezekiel. Not like I was ever going to share that song with the crew. I wanted to represent with something a little harder. I hoped she didn't suspect that it was all for EZ. I only spoke to her the other day 'cause she was his sis and all. But now that she came through in class, everything was different.

Not being able to look her in the eyes, I said, "I guess I owe you that. What do you want to know?"

"What's your stage name?"

I let out a huge sigh of relief because I knew she would've been able to see through my lies.

"MC Patria is my placa."

"So what, you're into all that patriotic red, white and blue stuff?"

"No, it's out of respect for where my parents come from, Puerto Rico. *Patria* in Spanish means 'homeland.' My father made me read this book about how Puerto Rico was stolen first by the Spanish and then by the United States. It's my way of claiming my country. Shit, Puerto Ricans on the island can't even vote for president of the United States because the island is a commonwealth."

"What's that?" she asked.

"It means we're neither a state or a country. We're homeless."

"Kind of like Black folk being stolen from their homes," she said.

"Yeah, I guess so."

I thought it was deep that Sadie could ask questions about what she didn't know without being self-conscious. I was also happy to let her know that I wasn't Mexican. There's nothing wrong with being Mexican. It's just when you speak Spanish and are brown everyone in Frisco be thinking you're Mexican. Our music was different and Puerto Ricans don't even like spicy food. My papi once told me that if you didn't live in New York or Chicago folks didn't even know what being Puerto Rican was until Ricky Martin and Jennifer Lopez blew up. And if they did, it was probably from watching a movie like *West Side Story* where most of the actors that played Puerto Ricans were White anyway. I used to get bored of Papi's lectures when I was a child, but what I wouldn't do to have him back home telling me his stories. I smiled to myself as I noticed that I was becoming just like him.

"Now that's what I'm talking about," she said.

"What?"

"I like seeing you smile."

Sadie suddenly made me self-conscious and I tried my hardest to stop smiling. But the way she looked at me made all my anger go away. For a second I didn't feel so guarded. And it felt good to be in the know after weeks of feeling like I didn't know shit.

"You be getting A's in Mrs. Hillaire's algebra class, right?" I said.

"Yeah, so what?"

"Well, do you think maybe you could help me out?"

"You mean tutor you?" she said.

"Yeah."

"Only if you help me with my lyrics, which I must admit aren't as sappy as yours," she said.

"Don't let those lyrics fool you. My stuff is usually more about the barrio or struggle," I said.

"Yeah, 'cause you're all hard. Gimme a break!"

I just couldn't get mad at her for calling out the truth. I'd become a sap over a man, something I promised myself I would never do after seeing my mom lose it over my dad. I started to get down on myself.

Sadie gave me a little push forward and put her arm around my shoulder like we had been girls forever. I felt so comforted by her touch that I totally forgot about Ezekiel and just focused on how good it felt to have a real homegirl again.

"I'm glad we're friends and you're gonna love my homegirl when you meet her," said Sadie.

"You're gonna love my girl Liza too," I said.

I stared at her hand as it was resting over my left shoulder. Her fingers were long and brown. We got a few stares as we walked down the hallway, but I didn't care 'cause I knew we were only girls. Nothing more, nothing less.

CHAPTER 7

THREE'S A CROWD

I didn't know you could have a real house in the hood. Sadie lived in the Bayview district. That's not far from me, but when I looked at her house it felt like she lived in another world. Her house is two stories high with a two-car garage and a huge backyard. We only rode one bus to get there, the 14 Mission. Her house is where Silver Avenue meets Bayshore Boulevard. It's mad nice. It's a mansion compared to my rundown apartment building.

Sadie rushed into the house. I was almost afraid to touch the door as I entered. Throughout the living room there were African statues with their naked breasts and big butts. I just kept staring.

"That's Yemaja the Yoruban goddess of birth and fertility," said Sadie. "Mother is obsessed with Africa even though she's never been there. Her church friends freak out over these statues. They think it's pagan and not Christian. But my mother ignores them, knowing she lives according to the Scriptures and in the end she only answers to God."

Then I noticed the huge cross over the fireplace and a picture of the Last Supper—except Jesus and the Apostles were Black, instead of White like in my mother's picture. Pictures of the Matthews family were also everywhere. There was this dorky picture of Sadie in her choir robe, and of course, Ezekiel's many hip-hop awards were scattered around the room. You could feel the love in the Matthews house.

Sadie came back from the kitchen with a bag of double-stuffed Oreos and some iced tea. As we were heading upstairs, Ezekiel entered with Ms. J-Ho herself and they were holding hands and acting all lovey-dovey. I guess they made up. I wanted to puke.

EZ was surprised to see me. "Oh Mariposa, what are you doing here?"

"Like that's any of your business," said Sadie. She grabbed my arm and rushed me upstairs. I felt like a kidnapped child. I didn't even get to say hello. There I was face-to-face with EZ for the first time since the other day in the cafeteria, and Sadie had to ruin it.

"What up, EZ. Gotta hit the books," I said, unable to take my eyes off J-Ho putting her arms around his waist and squeezing him close. That should be me, not her. We entered Sadie's room and she slammed the door.

Sadie's room looked like she was the child of some famous R&B artist. She had her own turntables, a flat-screen television and a huge queen-size bed. My small twin bed would look dwarfed next to hers. She even has a G5 computer with the latest music equipment so we could create our own beats. I have an old word processor that my moms got from a garage sale. I'm not trying to be a hater, but she's lucky.

Sadie and I sat on the bed and made Oreo triple decker sandwiches. It became a competition to see who could get the tallest sandwich into their mouth. I won hands down.

"I guess you got the bigger mouth," said Sadie. "You got a little filling in the corner of your mouth." She leaned closer and wiped it clean with her napkin, staring at me with her obsidian eyes. Learned that word in English class!

I never noticed how pretty Sadie was until she was less than a foot from my face. She had this perfect complexion that was zit free, with this red undertone and high cheek-bones that made me think she could be mixed with Native American. We just sat there for what seemed to be hours. My hands became a little clammy and I shifted back a little.

"I've been meaning to tell you something," said Sadie.

"I'm listening."

"You might feel differently about me when I tell you."

"Sadie, us being girls isn't gonna change. You had my back today and I don't forget those things."

"Well . . ." But before Sadie could finish what she was saying, Ezekiel barged through the door. Sadie jumped to her feet like we were under some type of terrorist attack. While I started to drool over how sexy he looked in his muscle T-shirt, which showed off his tight six-pack. I'd never seen it before, 'cause he always wears his clothes baggy.

"I can't find my new hoodie. Did you borrow it?" said Ezekiel.

"Why would I want your stinky clothes when your room smells like a men's locker room?"

"Well, it wouldn't be the first time."

"Get out of my room, and next time knock," said Sadie, slamming the door.

Going for the last jab, Ezekiel cracked open the door enough to peek his head in. "Butterfly, tell me if you need any help. Sadie smart but she ain't all that."

Before I could utter a word, Sadie cut in like she was marking her territory. "Well, solve this problem: one plus one equals two, and three is a crowd. So be gone. Go, disappear. This house is not the EZ fan club."

"I just want to know where my hoodie is, Sadie, I know how you be cross-dressing," said Ezekiel, laughing uncontrollably.

Sadie suddenly got hella pale. It was kind of a messed-up thing for EZ to blurt out. "You better shut your freakin' mouth or I'm gonna tell Mom that Jessica isn't the first hoochie you've brought up in this house."

J-Ho began calling for EZ. "EZ, I need your help with this next equation." I guess being alone with her huge ego was too much for even her.

Ezekiel began making faces at Sadie so she would shut up. "You're lucky she can't hear you." He was pissed and I had a feeling that if J-Ho hadn't called him, he and Sadie might've duked it out.

Reluctantly, EZ left without a word, but his face had one of those wait-until-later looks.

The doorbell rang and Sadie left me alone in her room as she ran downstairs to answer it. I don't think I've ever seen someone stand up to EZ like that before. Though I think Sadie is dope, I was kinda mad that she pushed him out. Then I heard the volume of the music in EZ's room go higher. My mind started wondering if EZ and J-Ho were really studying. They're probably kissing and feeling each other up. What I would do right now to be the one alone in that room with him, kissing that beautiful body of his, losing my virginity to the man of my dreams. That's a big thing for me, because my mom raised me to not give it up until I was married. But my hormones were raging and I just hoped in my heart that Ezekiel's missing hoodie was probably an excuse to say hi to me.

"Uh, earth to Butterfly? Can you come out of your cocoon so you can meet DJ Esa?"

Besides EZ, I usually get real mad at anyone who
called me by the English translation of my name. I only
let people close to me call me that. I could curse my mom
right now for naming me Mariposa. What parent names
her child after an insect? How can I ever get street cred
sounding like a hippie? "Butterfly" is right up there with
names like River or Summer. But Sadie is my girl so it's
all cool.

Once Sadie had my attention she introduced me to
her friend. "Evita, this is Mariposa, the dope emcee I was
telling you about."

Evita just stood there holding her violin case. She
stared at me like I wore the scarlet letter like Hester
Pryne in Hawthorne's book. What's a violinist doing tryin'
to be down with hip-hop anyway?

"I'm sorry, Sadie, I can't be down with this group if
she's in it," I said.

"I know you two have had issues, but I figured for the
sake of the talent show we could set everything aside,"
said Sadie.

"How could I not know her, you talk about her all the
time. Plus, the *pocha* is in my Spanish class," said Evita.

"What's a *pocha*?" asked Sadie.

"A *pocha* is someone that's brown on the outside, but
acts White," said Evita.

"At least one of us is brown," I said.

Sadie glared at Evita. "The only person hangin' with

White people in this room is you, Evita. I've seen you with that fake Bethany Doll. So don't front."

Although I'm glad that Sadie called her out, I just can't be down with that phony Evita. "The only reason I don't beat your butt right now, Evita, is I'm in Sadie's house, and unlike you, I have home training."

I really wanted to slap that smirk right off Evita's face, but out of respect for Sadie I kept my distance. I don't have to prove my Latinaness to the likes of her. My parents didn't teach me, so that's not my fault. And then the big one, which I could never change—you look Black, not Latina. Screw you, I love my dark skin. And I know everyone else does too. Otherwise they wouldn't be racing to those cancerous fake-and-bake tanning booths or paying loads of money to get those orangey-looking spray-on tans. I even read in *Honey* magazine that straight-hair girls can now get extensions that look like black hair. So much for not wanting to be Black or trying to copy our flava.

"Well, I like you both so you're going to have to figure out a way to get along," said Sadie. "Evita is my oldest friend, we've been girls since junior high. I was here when she first came to this country and no one wanted to talk to her because she didn't speak English. Remember how Bethany used to tease you, Evita?"

"You all went to the same school as Bethany? But she's rich," I said.

"Bethany is not rich. Her mother is a nanny for this rich family in Pacific Heights and Bethany gets the daughter's hand-me-downs and they live in the servant quarters. Their address gets them into the better schools. I went to the school 'cause my mother was the principal and Evita was there because her father was the janitor and they had a good bilingual curriculum," said Sadie.

"Yeah, Sadie's mom made Sadie hang out with me and we've been friends ever since," said Evita. "Maybe I misjudged you, Butterfly." She reached out, waiting for me to pound her fist. But when she mocked my name it made me think that the beef between Evita and me wasn't over.

I wanted to call her out, but as my grandmother used to tell me, keep your friends close and your enemies closer. "For the sake of winning this talent show, I'm cool if you are," I said. After all, we don't have to be homies to work together.

Sadie patted me on the back, but didn't do the same for Evita. I know Evita noticed because she looked sadly away and began setting up the turntables to avoid eye contact. I recognized that sad look, 'cause I've been feeling that way a lot lately whenever I see EZ with J-Ho. Maybe she's jealous. Well, good. I'm tired of always caring about other people.

"Great. Where's your homegirl?" said Sadie.

"Oh, Liza's always late," I said.

"Liza? You mean that tomboy who's dating that ice-head Rio?" said Evita.

"You don't even know her. Have you even spoken with her?"

"She's probably all strung out with her boyfriend. Let's start practice. We don't need her. She's just a dancer," said Evita.

"A b-girl. And I'm not in without her," I said.

"We need Mariposa, and she comes with her girl Liza. When did you become so mean? It doesn't become you, Evita. It's not you. Why you gotta be so judgmental? Just chill," said Sadie.

"Oh, so it's like that now," said Evita. "Some new girl enters our cipher and you kick me to the curb."

"You're just not acting right," said Sadie. "Mariposa didn't do anything to you."

I decided to just watch for once because I knew the more I said, the deeper I would fall. Ugly always showed its face and there's something about Evita I didn't trust. Evita was two-faced. She hadn't liked me from the start. It was her light-skinned issues, I knew it.

"Plus, talking about White girls, Liza's White," said Evita.

"Liza's half-Filipina and half-White," I said. "Plus, she looks more colored than you."

Someone knocked at the door. "Come in," yelled Sadie.

It was Mrs. Matthews, who was really tall and very regal. She looked like she just came from work in her gray wool suit. Sadie looked just like her mother.

"Your friend Liza is here. I was just showing her up and brought you all something to eat." Mrs. Matthews brought us a huge plate of homemade cookies and some soda, which she left on Sadie's desk.

"Thanks, Ma, for knocking. EZ barged in earlier and didn't even bother to knock," said Sadie. "Ma, this is my new friend Mariposa."

"Oh, the one your brother couldn't stop talking about last summer?"

Sadie looked disappointed, but I was happy that EZ spoke about me with his mother.

"Nice to meet you, Mrs. Matthews," I said.

"You too, sweetie." She looked to Sadie. "Where is your brother? I checked his room, and he wasn't there."

"He's in his room studying with Jessica."

"He's what? Oh no. This is the Lord's house, and he knows better than to bring some girl up in here without my being home."

Sadie just smiled to herself as Mrs. Matthews rushed out the door searching for EZ. I had to laugh too 'cause I'm sure Mrs. Matthews will never feel the same about J-Ho again.

Liza walked into the room and helped herself to cookies like she hadn't eaten in months. She stopped long enough to notice us all staring at her. "I left some for you all," said Liza, still stuffing her mouth.

I eyed the three cookies left. "That's rude, Liza. You just met Sadie and now you're eating all her food?"

"What's rude is how Sadie told on EZ," said Liza.

"Well, he deserved it. You should have seen him earlier before you came, putting my business out in public," Sadie said.

"J-Ho will be lucky if she ever steps foot in this house again," I said.

Sadie's face went from pride to guilt. "No loss to me. She used me once to get with my brother for the Twirp dance. I thought she wanted to be my friend."

Twirp is the annual dance where the girls are supposed to ask the boys out. I think the dance's concept is outdated nowadays 'cause girls ask the boys out as often as the boys ask us out. Still, I wouldn't have had the courage to ask EZ to Twirp.

"Why else would a senior want to be friends with a freshman?" said Evita.

"I thought maybe she liked me. Whatever. What does it matter? We're all here now, so let's practice for the talent show. All we need now is a name and a commitment to practice regularly so we can win this talent show."

"No offense, but I haven't even heard Mariposa rap," said Evita.

She probably thought I was going to mess up like I

did in Spanish class. Little did she know that I lived for hip-hop.

"That's fair. I'll spit and you show me what you got, Mizzzz DJ."

"DJ Esa," said Evita.

I began to pace like a boxer as Evita finished setting up her DJ equipment. Sadie looked relieved that I didn't cop an attitude. Once I thought she was ready, I cued Evita, or DJ Esa as she liked to be called, and launched right into my new song, "The Life."

It's the life that I choose or rather the life that chose me,
Nobody seems to know they own history.
So I put it together, solved it like a mystery
Boricuas in effect, you know I represent
Trying to make a dollar out of fifteen cents.
It's hard to survive and still pay the rent
Single mothers raising kids on their own,
Babies crying because the fathers not coming home.

This is the life in the barrio
strugglin' every day to survive yo
but hip-hop keeps it alive tho.

This is the life in the barrio
strugglin' every day to survive yo
but hip-hop keeps it alive tho.

The future might be bleak, but speak your mind and
    don't retreat.
Unity in the community is what we seek, I stand strong
    I'm not weak.
Tomorrow is never promised but today is here, let me
    kick it to your ear.
I'm gonna make it real clear before this cipher disap-
    pears.
Love is power, but people turning to hate is sour
Watch my creativity devour all the pain, and turn it
    into rain
Wash it all away because the revolution is today,
And like Assata Shakur I'm here to pave the way.

By the second line of the chorus, Sadie chimed in. Surprisingly, Evita was really feeling the music too. I must admit
Evita worked Sadie's turntables and her skills allowed
her to mix in some soulful violin samples that made our
music distinct. Who would have thought that a violin vir-
tuoso would turn out to be such a good DJ?

The loop ended and Evita took off her earphones. "So
what do you think?" she asked, hovering over the key-
board.

"S'aight," said Sadie.

"All right?" said Evita and I together.

"Just joking, that was off the hook."

"I'm really feeling the beats and the lyrics so it was

easy to come up with some tight dance moves," said Liza.

"We really might win that talent show after all," said Sadie.

"Yeah, I will. But for now, just think, Missy Elliott's hip-hop camp here we come," I said.

Evita and I both beamed with pride. Then we both remembered that we didn't like each other and tried to play it cool. I may not trust her, but when we put our skills together the music we made really worked. Which surprised me 'cause we're both so different. Who would have ever thought we could create such great beats?

"For a name, how about the Sista Hood," said Sadie. "Who would have ever figured that when all of us are so different, we could actually be a crew?"

"I love it," said Liza.

"It's all right," said Evita. "But I already got a sister and it's too much work."

"It's a symbolic sisterhood," said Sadie.

"Yeah, *chicas* stickin' together," I said, knowing she wouldn't get it. "I'm cool with it. For real though, I really wasn't cool with being in any group called the Sista Hood with Evita. But I was feeling her when we played."

"Not to bust up the party, but if we're gonna win, we better get practicing," said Sadie. "Can we take it from the top?"

"Word," said the rest of us.

"And this time, I was thinking that if Evita piped in a

few more drumbeats and Sadie, you opened singing the first verse a capella then I could join in rapping 'cause my singing skills aren't like yours," I said.

"Hit it," said Sadie.

And that we did. Evita added in the drumbeats and when Sadie sang, hands down it rose to another level. Sadie and I had this chemistry that was mad intense, I've never connected with another artist like that, not even EZ.

We were so excited we just continued to play, becoming lost in our music.

"Can you give me that last line again, Mari?" said Evita.

"Sure. 'Wash it away because the revolution is today, and like Assata Shakur I'm here to pave the way.'"

Sadie just began to freestyle her harmonizing. Evita added in a beat from her synthesizer. Liza kept spinning around doing moves that I would never be limber enough to perform. And somewhere during that six-hour rehearsal we became a group, despite our differences. It felt like magic. For the first time, I believed we might actually do all right at those tryouts.

CHAPTER 8

MAKING AMENDS

The bell rang. "Mariposa, will you stay after class?" said Señora Rivera as she passed out everyone's quizzes except mine.

Bethany and Evita got all excited as they got theirs back with a big 100 in red at the top. Mine finally came back with a big fat 65 and a capital D on the front.

Evita looked back and noticed my grade. "Bummer. It's probably all that talent show practice. You didn't have a lot of time to study."

"No, F's are for people who don't study. D's are for stupid people, duh?" said Bethany.

"This was an A and B conversation, so see yourself out, Bethany," said Evita.

Bethany looked hella surprised when Evita spoke back to her. Me too. I guess over the past week at practice we'd bonded a little and she was starting to open up to me.

Bethany winced from the force of Evita's words. I don't know if it was from pure shock that she stood up to her or that her ego had been hurt. Maybe a little of both. "Well, I guess this is a Mexican bonding thing. Can we go now? We have minions to tutor in the library," said Bethany.

"First, neither of us are Mexican. I've been telling you for months that my family is from Nicaragua. And Mari has told you she's Puerto Rican so many times she's starting to sound like a broken record. I told you Mari and I had practice for the talent show and I wouldn't be able to tutor this week." Everyone in class gasped from the shock that Evita finally spoke back to Bethany. Even she seemed surprised by the quickness of her own tongue.

We all waited for Bethany's response. But she just stood there with her arms crossed, waiting for Evita. "Maybe we should talk outside, I don't think I heard you correctly."

"No, you should go ahead alone," said Evita.

Bethany looked around, but all the students had left the classroom. Poor Bethany looked real nervous about having to exit without any ducklings. I guess the best target practice was payback. Still, I kind of felt bad for her sorry ass as she slung her Prada bag over her shoulder and walked out like a true loner.

After Bethany walked out I approached Señora Rivera's desk. "You wanted to speak with me?"

"Mariposa, I'm a little concerned about your performance in my class. You're a smart girl, but this is a difficult class and you must study. I keep trying to call your house, but either no one is there or they don't return my calls. Is there anyone at home who can help you? Your dad? I assume at least he's Latino with a last name like Colón."

"My parents are divorced," I told Señora Rivera. "And my mother works all the time."

"Well, there's tutoring in the library after school. I'm sure Bethany could help you."

"I can't, I have talent show practice."

"I'm sorry, Mariposa, but if you don't bring your grade up in my class you won't be able to participate."

Before I could utter what would have been a very defensive response, Evita said, "I can tutor her after talent show practice, Señora Rivera. This way everyone will be happy."

"Since Evita is such a good student, I'll agree. But I must see some improvement on your next quiz."

"Word," I said, then noticed Señora Rivera's confusion. "I mean, cool, thank you."

· · ·

Evita and I waited for Sadie at her locker after school. She looked happy to see us together as she began to walk quickly toward us. "Look at the two of you, hanging out like true homegirls."

"I wouldn't go that far, but we're cool, right?" said Evita.

"Evita was the bomb, yo, in class today. She gave Bethany her walking papers."

Sadie looked surprised. "You cut it off with her?"

Evita stopped slumping her shoulders and stood up proud. "Yeah, I got tired of her BS. I miss you, Sadie, didn't realize how much till we all started rehearsing for the talent show."

"Wow, I'm floored. I had given up on us."

It was great that Evita stopped wasting her time with Bethany, but all this chitchat back and forth was a little too much for me. "Can we stop talking and get walking? Evita promised to tutor me after rehearsals."

"Aren't we waiting for Liza?" asked Sadie.

"I guess she'll meet us at my house. I left a message on her cell," I said.

"Yeah, come to think about it, she wasn't in class today. Is she always this flaky?" said Evita.

"Always, no. Lately, yes. Rio occupies all her time."

We arrived at my bus stop and all jumped on.

The entire bus ride home nobody really talked. Evita

and Sadie just kept stealing looks at each other like two star-crossed lovers that had been reunited. No, not Sadie. Shit, maybe it's because I was right. Evita had done more than end her friendship with Bethany, she broke up with her.

I had never really taken a good look at Evita. Her eyes were hazel, and her tortoiseshell glasses gave her this intellectual mystery. Her hair was this sandy brown color and she had these straight bangs that hung right above her eyebrows.

Sadie sat next to Evita with her long, thin pianistlike fingers resting on the nape of her back. She had broad shoulders for a girl, to carry her developing breasts. The rest of her body was like her fingers, long and toned. My eyes couldn't stop focusing on her hands. And I started wondering what it would be like to hold them in mine.

"Twenty-fourth Street, here's our stop, *rucas*."

Evita and Sadie broke their bubble to exit the bus with me.

We arrived at my apartment and all I could hear was this melancholic tango music that my mother loved to play when she was sad. They both stopped at the front door. "You sure do have a lot of plants," said Sadie.

"It reminds me of my house," said Evita. "Almost like our parents are trying to re-create their homeland in the barrio."

I nodded. "It makes my mom feel safe." I left out the fact that if it weren't for me watering them since my father left they would be dead.

"You all hungry?" I rushed to the kitchen to clean up any empty wine bottles that my mother might have left out. Then I grabbed the only thing left to snack on, Oreos.

I passed the Oreos to the girls. "Sorry they're not double stuffed, my mom hasn't been shopping in a few weeks. That's all I could find."

"That's cool," said Sadie. "They're my favorites."

"I know," Evita said as she grabbed the entire package. She and Sadie sat on the couch and proceeded to make Oreo sandwiches.

"Mariposa, is that you," my mother slurred from her bedroom.

"Yeah, Mom," I yelled. "I'm here with the girls to practice, remember?"

"Can you keep it down. I got a huge headache and I need to get ready for work in two hours."

Sadie and Evita looked weirded out by the sound of my mother's voice. Me, I was just embarrassed that she decided to get drunk in front of my friends. That's why I never bring anyone home. But my mom has been a lot better lately, so I thought it would be cool.

"*Nena,* can you come here for a second?" said Mom.

I rushed to my mom's room. Her makeup was smeared from crying and she looked like a Mack truck had just ran over her face. "Your father called today. Finally admitted to me that he loved that woman and he wanted a divorce."

I didn't know what to feel in that moment. Divorce felt so final. "Everything is going to be fine, Mami. You'll see."

I found a few Tylenol with codeine in the bathroom cabinet and gave them to my mother for her headache. I rubbed her head as she swallowed them. "Don't worry, Mami. I'll always have your back."

"I know, *nena*. You take good care of me."

"Now get some sleep, we'll stay in the living room."

"You know I loved him."

"Yeah, I know, Mami."

"Will you call him and tell him that for me?"

"We'll see." I watched her as she drifted off to sleep, wondering if Mami ever told Papi that she loved him. I don't ever remember her saying those words to him. She could be very stingy with her affections at times.

Once Mami was asleep, I picked up the phone and dialed Papi's cell number. When he was living with us, he always answered my calls. Now I just seem to get his voicemail. But I didn't want to call him at home, talking to that homebreaker girlfriend of his would've pissed me off. "You've reached Alejandro Colón, please leave a message."

"Papi, can you give me a call? It's been a while and I would sure love to hear your voice. Mami's not doing so well. Umm. Guess that's it. Peace." I hung up the phone and wanted to cry but couldn't. Suddenly, I felt small and unsafe. I sucked up my tears and returned to my crew. Hoping that my mood would change for the better.

Sadie and Evita had their schoolbooks open and seemed oblivious to anything but their pencil fight. They kept taking, trying to break each other's pencils.

Sadie snapped her pencil hard onto Evita's, finally breaking it. "Show me the money," said Sadie as she stood up in victory.

"When you find it, make sure you share a little with your homegirls," I said.

"Listen, Mari, we don't have to practice today, we're in good shape for tomorrow's tryouts," said Sadie.

"Yeah, plus it's more important that you study for that Spanish quiz tomorrow," said Evita.

"If I would have known, I would've suggested we practice elsewhere."

"How about getting over yourself and opening that Spanish book before my father starts blowing up my cellphone to come home," said Evita.

"Yeah, her pops thinks she's tutoring at the library, remember?" said Sadie.

I took my Spanish book out of my backpack. I opened the book. Evita began explaining the conjugation of the different tenses. Only she made a lot more sense than Señora Rivera, and the Spanish words she used were a lot more like the ones I heard at home when my parents spoke Spanish. She explained each tense and then stopped and asked a question. She waited till I got it, then she went on to the next exercise. And finally I understood that stupid future perfect tense.

It seemed like we had only been studying for a few minutes when Evita's cellphone rang.

"Yes, Papi, I'm almost done. I'll be home in time to watch Sylvia, don't worry."

Evita gathered her stuff, hugged us both good-bye, then left. Leaving Sadie and I alone.

"Are you all right?" asked Sadie.

I just stood in front of Sadie feeling lost and inadequate. The only thing I felt was anger at my parents. "I'm fine. How about we forget about this homework thing and watch a movie? I went to Hollywood Video and rented a flick."

Sadie's eyes lit up. "Yeah, could use a break. What did you get?"

"It's from the late nineties, it's called *All Over Me*."

"Never heard of it. But then we were in elementary school then, right?" she said.

"Word. It was recommended on gurl.com. It's about friendship and coming out."

I looked at Sadie, but she didn't even flinch.

I popped the movie in and dimmed the lights in the room so we could have a real movie experience. When I reached for the Oreos, my pinky finger accidentally swiped against Sadie's. Touching her popped off all these feelings inside that confused me. It was like I had butter-flies inside my stomach. I tried to ignore the energy between us, but another part of me didn't want to fight it anymore. So I reached into the bag again, but Sadie's hand was gone and she was now all into the movie.

The film was at a part where the girls were kissing. I took a deep breath and looked over at Sadie, who couldn't take her eyes off the screen. It didn't mean anything, maybe she was freaked out by the girls getting together. Or maybe she doesn't like me like that now that Evita's back in her life.

I tried to clear my mind and think of EZ. But I couldn't stop my heart from pounding like a ticking bomb. Something in me just wanted to hold her hand. To feel her fingers entwined with my own. My palms were clammy and moist. Sadie seemed oblivious to what was happening to me.

On-screen the girls were now kissing each other all over. I placed my hand on top of Sadie's, she didn't move away but she didn't engage my hand either. At that exact moment, Sadie turned to me. Her eyes pierced my heart and I wanted to explode with everything that had been building up inside me. She leaned toward me, inspecting every inch of my face. She made the cutest little pout with her lips. I could finally hear her own heart pounding too. I smelled the vanilla filling from the Oreos coming from her heavy breath.

Then I did it, I kissed her. Full lip-lock. No pulling back now. I just melted in her arms as we made out for what seemed to be hours.

"What the hell is going on here?" said Mami. She just stood there staring at us in the dark like Lurch on *The Addams Family*.

We quickly pulled away. Moving to opposite ends of the sofa, I said, "We were practicing for the talent show?"

What a stupid response, I thought to myself. Mami just stood there not believing a word of my stupid lie. Sadie and I sat there frozen, afraid to move for fear of my mother's wrath. The silence was so uncomfortable, the only thing we could hear was the sounds of car alarms going off in my neighborhood.

"I think Sadie should leave," said Mami.

Sadie gathered her things without uttering a word. She opened the door and left as quickly as possible.

I now stood face-to-face with my mother. And all she could say was, "Lock the door after me, I gotta go to work."

Once Mami left, I picked up the phone and dialed Liza's home number. No one answered, so I decided to call her cell.

"Hello?"

"Liza, it's Mari. Do you have a moment to talk?"

I have to say I was happy that Liza picked up the phone, I half expected her not to be there.

"Mari, I'm sorry about not making rehearsal, but I had to help my mother with the grocery shopping."

"Are you home now?"

"Yes. My mother is in the other room."

I wanted to bust her out about why no one picked up, but being outed by my mother seemed like a bigger issue at the moment.

"I don't know who to turn to."

"About what?"

"Sadie and I kissed and my mother caught us."

"I thought you were straight."

"I am. I mean, I was."

"Did you like it?"

"Yes."

"Then you're at least bisexual or questioning."

"But, I still love EZ."

"Sounds like you're confused," said Liza.

"Liza, this isn't helping. You're only telling me what I already know. I should go, we'll talk later."

"You sure?"

"Yeah," I said.

After getting off the phone with Liza, I got undressed, grabbed Gizmo in my arms and all I could think about was when I would get a chance to kiss Sadie again.

CHAPTER 9

THE AUDITIONS

I rushed from Spanish class to the auditorium for auditions, beaming as I held my quiz, which had a big B written across the top.

Sadie arrived with her bag loaded with books so she could study later. "Are you okay?"

"Yeah, I'm fine; are you?"

"Of course, I've been wanting to kiss you for a while. I enjoyed it till your mother busted in like some axe killer from a horror flick."

We both grinned. I have to admit mine came from a place of confusion and curiosity. I wasn't sure if I wanted Sadie and I to go anywhere. I don't really think I'm gay, just exploring. Gurl.com said that it's perfectly normal for teenagers to be curious about anything sex related. It's all about growing up.

Sadie looked at me with genuine concern. "I hope she didn't wile out too much? I kept jumping up every time the phone rung at my house last night. Thinking your mom would call my house and bust me out to my mom. Then we would have two psycho killers on our behinds."

"Word."

We both clammed up as Evita arrived with her violin in tow.

"What's up, my sistas?" said Evita.

I handed her my Spanish quiz to cover up the tension between Sadie and me. "All thanks to you!"

"You're very welcome. I couldn't take that sorry look on your face whenever Bethany scored higher than you."

"Me either."

Evita looked at Sadie and then to me. I was wondering if our awkwardness showed.

"Don't tell me she's late?" said Evita.

"Liza's always late," I said.

"She'll be here," said Sadie.

"And if not, we'll go on without her," said Evita.

"No, Liza not being here would be bad luck." Liza has been my good luck charm since the first time I took the mic for our fifth grade talent show. The two of us were like Salt 'n Pepa minus one, except I was the only one singing. I rocked the mic, but Liza helped us gain the respect of the dudes who had never seen a girl with her moves before. Together forever we promised on that day and until this year I never questioned that we would ever separate.

To make things worse, Ms. J-Ho entered with her male entourage, including Ezekiel. She had on this tight top and some Daisy Duke shorts, all for show, because it was rainy and cold outside. But the dudes were eating her up. She would do her little hip sway down the hall and one by one the dudes would get behind her like some follow-the-leader train. I had to watch this for ten minutes, then she pulled Ezekiel to her side, kissed him and slapped his butt.

"I told you not to do that, Jessica," said EZ all loud.

Jessica batted her eyes and eased up to EZ more submissive like. "I'm sorry, it's just so cute."

"Well, if you want to roll with me that stuff stops in public."

Jessica just gave him one of her "how dare you walk away from me" looks, then disappeared behind the stage.

Ezekiel stepped up onto the stage with Mr. Mintz and announced the order of the groups. We were going on after J-Ho and then Rio's crew would follow us. The auditorium was loud and the students were all hyped to perform and watch.

"Can Jessica join us backstage so we can do a mic check?" said Mr. Mintz.

Jessica danced up to the mic and blew Ezekiel a good luck kiss in front of the entire auditorium. "Okay, mic check, mic check. Girls wanna tease me, boys wanna get with me. My man knows there's only one me, don't hate on me for being free. 'Cause I didn't become Jessy-Ten for being ugly, I leave that to MC Patria a wannabe hottie."

EZ rolled his eyes at her. "All right, Jessy-Ten, thanks. The mic is working."

Then she wiggled her anorexic self onto the stage. Ezekiel and Mr. Mintz took their seats in the front row, along with our assistant principal Mrs. Hillaire and Mr. Leash, my history teacher.

"Mr. Matthews, who's MC Patria?" asked Mr. Leash.

"She was referring to Mariposa, that's her hip-hop name. An emcee is a rapper."

They all shook their heads but for some reason I think they still didn't get it.

"One love to the Sista Hood," yelled Ezekiel. Probably his attempt to not seem partisan toward J-Ho. Still, we all appreciated the love. J-Ho, however, rolled her eyes at Ezekiel.

Before entering the stage she turned to all three of us and said, "Break a leg, ladies! No, two."

Sadie stepped up to her and said, "Not before I break yours."

You gotta love Sadie. She tells it like it is. In that moment she was my hero.

As J-Ho walked onto the stage, EZ's fan club and by association hers began hollering, "Go J-Lo! Go J-Lo."

I turned to Evita and Sadie. "She probably bribed them with fantasies of getting with her if they were loud."

They laughed out loud. I hoped it would break J-Ho's flow. I admit, I was jealous. J-Ho just exuded confidence, something I didn't have when I had to be on. Every time I rocked the mic, I couldn't sleep the night before. And just before I go onstage, my stomach becomes nauseous from all the nervous energy. I looked around and still no Liza.

"All right, you all. Mic check," said J-Ho. Then she launched into her song "Street Cool."

I'm classy and fancy,
girls hate me because their mans romance me.
Size two frame with an ill tight game,
Before the song is over, you'll remember my name,
born and destined for fame.
But don't blame me because your rhymes are lame
Sweet like honey, and I definitely love money
Fellas love my style,
for me they go the extra mile,
all I have to do is wink and smile.

By now the crowd was wilding out. Why, I don't know. Her lyrics were simple and unoriginal. But J-Ho had this magical energy and she knew how to connect with the crowd. Then she moved to the front of the stage. She winked at all the guys and finished the song like she was flirting with each and every guy in the audience.

> *These boys are so cute but their minds are not ready,*
> *So here we go, because hip-hop is my steady.*
>
> *These boys are so cute but their minds are not ready,*
> *So here we go, because hip-hop is my steady.*
>
> *Let me slow it down, and turn it around,*
> *I got something cooking, but it's not for the looking.*
> *Smart and savvy, I know I could make you happy.*
> *Sing you songs and lullabies, because I think you fly.*
>
> *Talking sweet in my ear, I know you're sincere.*
> *Looking deep in my eyes made me realize,*
> *You ain't these other guys, me and you forever baby,*
> *we're always on the rise.*

She ended the final verse focused on Ezekiel, which made everyone jealous 'cause the boys wanted to be him and the girls wanted him. J-Ho had what every girl wanted: she was cool, beautiful and had the most popular guy in the entire school.

If I wasn't nervous enough before her crowd-pleasing performance, I was scared senseless now, 'cause Liza was a no-show. J-Ho stood on the stage soaking in her success, until Mr. Mintz came in to announce the next group up, which was, of course, the Sista Hood.

"You can go before us if you want," I said to the other group.

They just laughed and their lead singer said, "No, we'll wait our turn."

"Where is Liza?" I asked Sadie.

"I knew she wasn't good enough to be down with us. I told you, Sadie," said Evita.

"It'll be all right, we'll just rock it like we've been doing at rehearsals. You don't need Liza. Plus, heads are gonna really be feelin' our song. Not like that BS that J-Ho be spitting."

"So now we're ready for the Sista Hood. Introducing: MC Patria, Soul Siren, DJ Esa and Pinay-One," said Mr. Mintz.

Nobody clapped. Until Ezekial yelled, "Rock the mic, y'all." Then the audience clapped just to follow MC EZ.

We took our places on the stage. I looked out at all the people and for some reason I couldn't remember what to do. I froze, like a big giant icicle.

"Mariposa, just let it flow," whispered Sadie.

"See, I knew she'd mess it up," said Evita. Sadie motioned for her to be quiet.

I stepped forward ready to spit but my energy was mad scattered. Something was wrong. I lost my confidence.

So Sadie stepped forward. "Rock the mic. Soul Siren, MC Patria and DJ Esa in the house." Evita gave us a beat. The students hollered all kinds of boos.

"Forget MC Patria. It's MC Loser," yelled Bethany from the crowd.

"Yeah, with a capital L," said someone else.

Then Sadie just launched into the song, "The Sista Hood."

Who we are and where we come from is universal.

Sadie looked at me, pushing me to join in, but I was still paralyzed. Liza rushed onto the stage, late but she was here. But for some reason her moves were off and the magic we used to have disappeared. I launched into the song, but I wasn't feelin' it. And if I couldn't feel it I know the crowd thought it sucked.

When my pen hits the paper then it starts to bleed,
Everything inside of me, look in my eyes and see.
Working together, sticking it out,
because the Sista Hood is what we are all about.

People were walking out. Someone even threw an empty paper bag onto the stage. I made eye contact with Ezekiel and he just kept pounding his fist to his heart. But I couldn't go there in my typical MC Patria style. I really

was a loser with a capital L. I shut down, but Sadie saved
the day by just taking the lead and working the mic as I
remained mute. Evita chimed in with these electronic hip-
hop violin beats and I must admit she and Sadie created
magic.

> *We're gonna stick together, we'll make it through the*
> *weather,*
> *Savvy and clever but where do I start?*
> *No one taught you how to protect your heart,*
> *Look good and still be smart,*
> *So you're playing a role, stuck in a part.*

I finally chimed in at the chorus, but this was obviously
now the Sadie and Evita show. Liza was doing moves that
we never rehearsed, and she was totally offbeat. We finished the song.

> *The options are there if you choose to care*
> *Just believe in yourself and you're almost there.*

> *The options are there if you choose to care*
> *Just believe in yourself and you're almost there.*

> *Let go of the secrets that you guard deep inside,*
> *It will make you feel good and walk with pride.*
> *Betrayal deception, lies and rumors,*

Kill the truth and grow all kinds of nasty tumors.
Our bond is strong, like the Energizer Bunny it will
  always last long.
The Sista Hood is where we belong, nothing can do us
  wrong.
With true admiration and integrity
ladies of the mic, destroy negativity.

Sadie sang the last word and the crowd just yelled, "Soul Siren and DJ Esa!" MC Patria and Pinay-1 were far from their minds. I ran off the stage and Liza followed. As we passed Rio and his crew, he had this grin of satisfaction that I just wanted to smack off his face. He didn't even console Liza, who had choked too.

"Mariposa, wait. I'm so sorry I was late. But—"

"I don't want to hear it Liza. It's all your fault that I froze. You always be thinkin' about yourself."

We were now standing face-to-face as Rio and his group were preparing to enter the stage. I noticed Liza had this bruise on her upper lip. She probably fell or something and, frankly, I didn't care.

Liza attempted to pull me back.

"Liza, I need a kiss for good luck," Rio said.

I know there was probably a good reason as to why she was late, but I just didn't want to hear it.

"I just want to know one thing. Which group are you a part of? Ours or his?"

"Don't do this, Mari. Please don't make me choose."

"Liza, get over here," he said.

"Go comfort the crackhead," I said.

Then I walked off alone. Not caring about anything but nursing my deeply wounded ego.

CHAPTER 10

THE SLEEPOVER

I didn't want to go, but Sadie insisted that both Liza and I come to a sleepover at her house on Friday to celebrate our making it into the talent show. I had cooled down a bit after the audition, but I was still mad at Liza. The only reason we got into that talent show is because Sadie saved the show and Ezekiel believed in us. Still, I wouldn't have blamed Sadie for kicking Liza and me out of the group. Part of me wished she would have given me my walking papers. It would have been easier that way.

Evita couldn't come because she had to watch her little sister. For once, I really missed her. I'd actually grown to like her, and I could see why she and Sadie were friends.

Liza called after the audition and apologized again. We

talked more about Sadie and me, but I was done with her. I didn't want to give in this time to her little stunts. She seemed all smiley tonight. She and Rio probably had some good sex.

Sadie poured me some of her mother's virgin daiquiri mix and I just sat there sipping my drink, watching as Liza and Sadie bonded over an autographed picture of Crazy Legs from Rocksteady, this old school b-boy crew from the Bronx.

"My dad's younger brother used to run with him and Davey D," said Sadie.

"Your pops knew Rocksteady?"

"Back in the day hip-hop was about the people and they took it to the streets," said Sadie.

Liza couldn't keep her eyes off the picture. "Wow, it says 'To Ezra M, the dopest older brotha I could ever have.' The only thing I ever got from my pa were these crazy cards."

"My pa isn't famous or nothin'."

"Yeah, but he has the connects," said Liza.

Sadie took the photo off the wall and handed it to Liza.

"Here, you take it. I think it's meant for you. Maybe it'll give you a little inspiration."

"No, that would get boosted where I live. You can't keep anything valuable at the North Beach projects," said Liza.

"Just take it," said Sadie.

"How about if I keep it here for safekeeping? And when I have a place for it I get it from you."

"Cool. It'll be waiting here for you."

I couldn't believe that Sadie was generous enough to give Liza something so special. And she'd just met her. Frankly, after our auditions, I wouldn't have given Liza anything.

"Okay, can you two kiss and make up, please." Sadie pleaded with us and I must admit she looked so cute and innocent. I had to smile. "See, there's the smile."

"Kiss her, eeewww," said Liza.

"All right, we all know you love your man."

"I'm really sorry, Mariposa."

Of course, I pouted. But a part of me knew that Liza never meant to be late. I knew she loved me. I just needed someone to be mad at, so I could save face.

"So . . ." I said, pouring each of us more of the yummy daiquiris and noticing a scar above Liza's eyebrow. "Liza, tell us what it's like, the first time?"

Liza looked shocked that I was talking to her again. And I knew that asking her about Rio would most likely allow us to reconnect. The evil twin side of me also knew that my question would make her feel awkward. But how could she not answer it? She had to make it up to me.

"Yeah, I'm kind of curious. Do share," said Sadie.

Sadie and I both waited for Liza's response as neither of us evidently had ever had sex. Liza had sex a couple of times even before Rio with her ex-boyfriend Rashid, who was this dope b-boy and friends with her older brother. This time I knew Liza loved Rio, though he's too self-absorbed or drugged out to notice how much she cares. In the past, she at least stayed true to hip-hop. Now her life revolved around when Rio wanted to see her and what he wanted to do. She never had time for anything else. I was surprised she was even staying over at Sadie's tonight.

"Well, it's kind of weird the first time," said Liza.

Sadie got a little anxious. "What do you mean?"

Liza looked at Sadie funny. She was uncomfortable sharing her business with her since they'd just met. "Well, you don't really know what to do."

"Figured as much. Sometimes I hear Ezekiel going at it with Jessica and it sounds like he's the only one getting excited," said Sadie.

"Maybe he's not feelin' Jessica," I said.

"No, he's just selfish. It would be the same with any other girl," said Sadie.

"Well, that's why I'm saving myself for Mr. Right," I said.

I just knew in my heart that it would be different if EZ and I made love. It would be the kind of lovemaking that songs are written about—electric, like in the movie *Love Jones*, where we couldn't keep our hands off or stop kissing because we just wanted to devour every ounce of each other. He would rise early the next morning and tell me he loved me.

"Earth to Mariposa?" Sadie reached over and flicked her finger against my earlobe.

"Hmm?"

"Do you think you could let a guy kiss you down there?" asked Sadie.

I really wanted to drift back to EZ, but friendship called. "Well, I don't know. Don't you think that's a real private thing?"

"Of course, but don't you think it would feel great? It always cracks me up in movies 'cause the guys are all moaning and most of the time the women are just laying on their backs waiting for it to be over. I'm always like, please her," said Sadie.

"I didn't get to finish," said Liza. "What I wanted to say is the first time stinks, but with Rio it's different. Maybe it's because I love him," said Liza.

Sadie was determined to prove her point. "Does he go down on you?"

"Well . . ."

"No, he doesn't, right?"

"Only because I don't let him," said Liza. "I don't even feel comfortable touching myself down there. I'm just happy with the way he feels inside of me."

"Well, *chica*, I hope you're using protection," I said.

" 'Cause your little lover is a huge mack. I wouldn't put it past him to cheat."

"Forget cheating. I know your man be doing hard-core drugs. You gotta watch out, girl," said Sadie.

Liza rolled her eyes, which made me want to take it all back. She really was in love and my dislike for Rio might have been the very thing that was pushing her and me apart. I understood how she was feeling, 'cause I felt that way about EZ.

All of a sudden Liza's cellphone rang, to the song "Shake Ya Tailfeather" by Nelly and Puff Daddy, P. Diddy or whatever he's calling himself these days. For the first time Liza didn't race to answer the phone.

"Yeah? I told you I was spending the night with my homegirls. I'm with Mariposa. I can't come now. Of course, I love you," she whispered. "Okay, fine."

I watched as Liza spoke with Rio and I knew once she got off the phone that she would leave us to be with him. I wanted to be wrong, but he had that effect over her. I wondered if I would be like that if I had a boyfriend. But dudes just don't feel me the way they feel Liza. She was more accommodating. I made them fend for themselves. Unless it was EZ, but sometimes even with him I caught an attitude. I knew I was hooked, but at least the entire world didn't know.

Liza got off the phone. "I gotta bounce. Rio needs me."

"You program your cell ringer to 'Shake Ya Tailfeather' 'cause that's what you do when he calls," I said.

"He's been there for me these past months, when you were at camp and God knows where else. He loves me for who I am, doesn't care if I'm White or Filipina. His boys gotta bit strung out and left him without any money to get home. I can't leave him stranded."

"Whatever, Liza. Rio does whatever he wants, when he wants. Then when he decides he has time for you, he snaps his fingers and expects you to jump," I said.

I'd grown tired of keeping my mouth shut. Even everyone at school knew Rio was a crystal meth head. Silence equals death and I really didn't want Liza to end up in some alley. "You sure he isn't using your money to buy more ice? You worry me, Liza. You're always late, sometimes you never show up at all. You don't even make it to class. And now you're giving him money that you don't have."

"I haven't known you real long, Liza, but you're always showing up with bruises. I just want you to know I'm here if you need to talk," said Sadie.

"Oh, those. They're just from me and my brother dancing. They can be a little rough. It's all play," said Liza.

"You've said that before," I said. "But answer me this—how come before Rio you never had bruises?"

Liza put on her shoes and gathered her things. "I wish you believed me, Mariposa. It would mean a lot to me if you and Rio could get along. But I'm not leaving him just because you think he's a loser. Maybe you need to look at your own confused life instead of always criticizing mine."

Then she turned to Sadie. "Cool chillin' with you, Sadie, and thanks for the Crazy Legs picture. That was sweet. Please tell your mom thanks for me. I'll be on time to our next rehearsal."

Liza gave Sadie a hug, then rushed past me without even a glance. She left me with a very empty feeling inside. She's my oldest and closest friend. I do love her. Who else is going to look out for her? Her mother was always working and her brothers were absorbed in their own lives. I wanted to tell her that I'll be there no matter what, but the words just didn't come out.

Sadie put her hand on my hand and began stroking my hair. Her presence was very calming. "It'll be all right. She'll come around. She just can't hear you right now."

"I just hope it isn't too late."

"I guess this group thing isn't going to be as easy as I thought," said Sadie.

"Maybe it's all my fault. I guess I just bring out the best in everybody," I said.

"No, you're just real about how you feel. And messing up at the auditions, well, I know that's a one-time deal. I know you got chops. The only reason I don't get stage fright is that I've been performing in my church choir since I was old enough to talk."

"You really feel that way?"

"Really," said Sadie. "I love how you never kiss up to

people. I noticed that about you the first time I saw you in the cafeteria."

"Oh, you mean the first time we spoke in the cafeteria?" I said.

"Girl, I noticed you the first day of school."

"What?"

"I couldn't stop talking about you to Evita."

"What did you say?"

"How mysterious you were as you sat alone, writing in that same black sketchbook you had in history class. Your bangs fell forward, slightly brushing against your cheek and it was as if nothing else mattered except what you were writing on that paper. You were mad intense and so beautiful."

"Oh, so that's what Evita meant when she told Bethany you couldn't stop talking about me. I thought you were mad dogging me."

"Yeah, I kept bugging Evita out, saying I knew we would be friends. She was like, not while I'm around. Then she got together with that Bethany Doll. Trying to get me all jealous."

"Did you?"

"Do I look jealous?"

As we sat on the bed, she just looked at me. Then she leaned over and kissed my cheek. Our fingers became entwined and we just explored each other's hands and bodies. Just touched and allowed our fingers to wander. Weird, huh? Dudes would have already been at third base. It felt new, exciting and scary all at the same time. Sadie just spooned me, her nose nuzzled in my neck.

It felt good to be touched. The last time that I felt this safe, I was ten. My dog Frisco died and my father just hugged me until I stopped crying.

CHAPTER 11

THE MORNING AFTER

I woke up at Sadie's and she was still sleeping soundly next to me. And all I could feel was panic. Trying to understand how I'd ever let things between us go this far. Did this mean I'm a lesbian? I never really thought I liked girls. I admit, I've appreciated another girl's body or good looks from time to time. I'll even be the first to say I love me some Mystic or Missy Elliott 'cause they're smart and not hooched out. But does that make me gay?

I felt like I wanted to puke. Why me? Why did Sadie decide to kiss me of all people? Do I look gay? I rushed over to Sadie's mirror. And I just stood there doing an inspection. I got beautiful, long curly hair. Not gay. I'm pretty, definitely not gay. I'm in shape. Well, could go either way. I love hip-hop. Gay. I'm strong. Gay. Well, it's a split, two to two with one either way. Does this make me bisexual? Hell no. I don't get freaky like that.

Like I don't have enough on my mind. I put on my pants and gathered my clothes, trying not to wake Sadie. As I made my way to the door, Sadie woke up with a huge smile.

"Hey sweetie, come over and give me a hug." She opened her arms, like she expected me to rush toward her like we were girlfriends.

"Not before you brush your teeth," I said.

"I didn't say a kiss," said Sadie as she rolled her eyes. I just stood there looking at her and not moving.

"All right, be that way." Sadie got up and headed to the bathroom, but not before she noted that my clothes were on and my backpack was already around my shoulders.

"I thought we were going to hang out today," said Sadie.

"I forgot that I had to do something with my mom."

"Last night you wanted space. And now you're itching to be near her. So it's like that?"

I had all this nervous energy and just wanted to leave. But then Sadie just looked at me and my heart softened. Sadie really is beautiful. Her eyes are so sincere. You can tell a lot by looking at someone's eyes. And I knew I couldn't just up and leave like some insensitive dude. Who would have thought that I could ever flee after the first night we ventured past first base. And Sadie wasn't just anyone. She was my friend. My homegirl. Maybe even my sister-in-law one day. Shit, what if she told EZ? It was just a kiss, no big deal, right? So why did it feel like so much more?

So I took a seat on the bed. "All right, you brush your teeth and I'll wait."

Sadie raced to the bathroom to freshen up. I sat there trying to figure out how in the hell I would get out of this drama. I was supposed to get with EZ, not his sister. My parents would freak. I remember one Sunday, we were coming from Denny's and we passed the Dyke March on Market Street and my dad just kept making stupid comments.

"All those freakin' dykes, they just need a real man. Probably never even had sex with a man," said Papi.

And the funny thing is my mom would just look at my father like he was the crazy one and say, "Like you should talk."

Papi just rolled his eyes at Mom and walked off like a wounded child. I never really paid it any mind, but I guess they were having problems even then. I know my father was wrong for saying all that stuff. But Papi saw race as always being more important and felt that who someone slept with was private. I guess it was all that good old Catholic brainwashing. Personally, I think someone should be able to love who they love freely.

Sadie came back all refreshed. She has this natural beauty, doesn't need any makeup or anything. A part of me wished I could just embrace what happened with Sadie and be fine. Another part of me was really afraid to even admit I could go there with a girl. Maybe I was just thirsty for some love.

"Mari," said Sadie, as she took off the T-shirt she wore to bed. Wow. Her boobs were perky and big. I couldn't stop looking at them. Sadie walked toward me on a mission. Our bodies were less than a foot apart. She reached her hand out and gently turned it around so she could read my palm. She traced the middle line that creased my palm with her finger.

"You know you have a long love line?"

"For real?"

She traced the middle line again. "This is your love line, and it's long. That means you'll have lots of love in your life."

"How do you know that?"

"Honestly, I have this obsession with hands. And I love hands that have scars or don't look perfect. Like your hands—they're always clammy when you're nervous, and they have hangnails from all that cuticle biting you do."

Sadie started to massage my fingers. Before I knew it her hands were interlocked with mine and she was pulling me toward her. And we kissed again. I kissed her too, but at least that time I pushed her away sooner.

"I can't take this right now, Sadie. You're my home-girl."

"Okay," said Sadie.

"Listen, I'm not gay."

"You're just nervous."

I was surprised that she was so agreeable. I assumed it would be more difficult. But Sadie just sat on her bed and then motioned for me to join her. I guess I expected that she would want to be girlfriends and start to do everything with each other. Girls can be like that when they're friends. I can only imagine what it's like when you're lovers. I joined her on the bed.

Sadie pushed my bangs away from my face and then I took a deep breath. "I like you as a friend, nothing more."

"Well, if we can't be girlfriends, then I don't think I can be your friend," said Sadie.

"Fine. Then maybe I should leave."

As I walked down the stairs of her house, Sadie yelled, "Mariposa, wait. I didn't mean it."

Part of me wanted to race back. To make it all better. Another part of me was afraid of all the feelings that I had brewing inside me. But another part of me was proud of myself for being honest about how I felt. I was glad that I spoke up, but for some reason it still felt like a disaster.

CHAPTER 12

THE AWAKENING

A big sign said FOR THE HOMELESS. There were clothing and book donations stacked throughout the hallway in boxes. Mrs. Matthews had organized a phone tree on Sunday to call all the parents in our school to donate items for her annual church clothing drive. Sadie and Ezekiel were spearheading the student effort at the school. Evita helped Sadie pack and mark boxes so that everything would be organized when time came for pickup. Evita seemed happier than I had seen her in a long time. She and Sadie seemed closer. EZ spoke to all the cute girls. I was surprised to see that J-Ho wasn't there to make sure that everyone knew she was EZ's girl. Most of the students walking by would have totally laughed at the effort, but having EZ there made everyone think it was cool.

I wanted to drop off my stuff, but I couldn't figure out how to do it without Sadie seeing me. If things would have been different, I would have been there right beside her, helping out for the cause. It's sad that most of the students in my school are more concerned about grades and appearances than they are about such a horrible event like Hurricane Katrina. Sadie and Ezekiel's organizing reminded me of my dad and all his talk of providing free lunches and other stuff he did for the community when he was in the Lords. I knew he would be so proud if he knew I was a part of doing something like this at Stanford.

I gathered my courage and walked toward Sadie. But then Evita looked up at me and rolled her eyes. Then her hand gently massaged Sadie's back and something inside told me I wouldn't be welcomed.

"Can you hand this to the people organizing the drive over there for me," I asked a girl I didn't even know.

"Someone might think I'd actually wear this," said the student. Then she saw Ezekiel, grabbed my bag and raced to make her donation. I turned away from my former friends and walked toward the window.

"Mariposa, I was looking for you," said Ezekiel. EZ walked toward me with his normal posse. He waved goodbye to them and approached me alone.

"Hey EZ," I said, turning my head away from the

window. "That's funny, I was just thinking about you." I looked down at my shoes, embarrassed suddenly. I wondered if Sadie had told him about us kissing.

"So, what were you thinking?"

"I don't know. You were passing through my mind. Just kind of floating through it," I said.

He was looking for *me*. Finally, after all these months he came to me, and I'm a little scared that it may be too late. After getting with Sadie, how can I ever look him in the eyes again? Love the brother, kiss the sister. What a jerk I am. I'm no better than my father. I really cared about Sadie, but she doesn't move me the way EZ does. I wanted to melt as he towered above me with his lean torso and cute butt.

"I wanted to talk to you when you were at the house, but my sister wouldn't let me near you."

"You're the one that wanted us to be friends. Now we are. So you're just gonna have to deal with it," I said.

"I see she must have gotten to you."

"What do you mean by that?"

"Turned you against me. I love my sister, but for some reason I get on her nerves," said Ezekiel.

"Probably because you're the golden child and can do whatever you want."

"What? Sadie is the baby. My mom thinks she's perfect."

"Yeah, but you're a boy so you get away with more.

You're both smart, you wouldn't be at this high school if you weren't. But let's be real—your parents are cool with you being a hip-hop head because you're a boy. But Sadie is supposed to be the good church girl and only sing in the choir."

Ezekiel kept looking at me, which made me feel mad self-conscious. "You have the most beautiful smile," he said softly. "You should use it more."

The bell rang and the hall started to empty and everything became quiet and dim. In the distance, I could hear a teacher talking and feet shuffling to class. His voice was muffled, like it was coming from behind a closed door. The late bell rang.

"Thank you," I said, looking directly into his eyes.

We were whispering now, but in the empty hallway our words seemed loud.

Ezekiel smiled. "I've missed you, MC Patria. I expected you to be helping Sadie out since the two of you have become so inseperable."

"Didn't think you noticed now that you have Jessica."

Ezekiel shrugged. "Yeah. Well, me and Jessica got issues."

I turned back to the window. "Really?"

After a moment he said "Mariposa" so softly, I could barely hear him. My name just rolled off his tongue and I must admit the sound of his voice made everything between my legs sweaty. I squeezed them together in an attempt to shut off all the raging feelings I had for him at that very moment.

"I miss talking with you. Jessica is beautiful and all, but she just doesn't pack a punch like you."

I guess him missing me should have made me feel good, but instead it really just made me feel second best. Always being the best friend without girlfriend benefits with boys gets old. And I wanted to be seen as beautiful too. What girl doesn't?

"Well, you're six months too late, Ezekiel."

All of a sudden, EZ stood up real tall. "I'm too late to be your friend?"

Oh, good one, Mariposa. I guess I just assumed since he and J-Ho were having problems that he was interested in me as a girlfriend. I thought maybe my card reading would come true. My love line would finally give me what I wanted.

Making a quick recovery, I said, "Friends stay in touch. They don't drop each other over some girl."

"Well, Jessica gets jealous of other girls. She thinks men and women can't be friends. She thinks you like me. And I'm like, give me a break, she's the same age as my sister."

Now I felt hurt. Guess I'm just too young. Maybe it was better this way. I just wished I could turn off my feelings for him. You like the brother. You make out with the sister. What does this make you, MC Patria? It makes you a two-time loser. Maybe I am a lesbian. A dyke, a *mari-macha*, and every man in the world can tell—so they stay away from me. Sadie said men can't deal with a strong sis-tah. If Sadie liked me half as much as I liked her brother, I gotta be careful. I don't have the heart to hurt her. She's such a good friend. I must make it up to her. But then, Ezekiel just stood there staring at me, my heart beating hard beneath my hoodie. I folded my arms across my chest wanting to quiet it, afraid he'd be able to hear it and laugh. I turned back to the window.

"You ever get scared, Mariposa?"

I swallowed. "Yeah." It was not supposed to be like this. This real. This close to who I was. Like he could see right through me kissing all over his sister and pining away for him at the same time.

Liza told me that being in love was like someone wrap-ping you inside of them, and that's what I feel like now. Like slowly I was being wrapped inside Ezekiel—inside his eyes, inside his voice, inside the way he talked about things when he was with me. EZ was just more real with me, something I didn't see him doing with many others.

"Like right now," he said.

"Yeah. I'm scared about a lot of things. Sometimes my mind just gets all mixed up about everything," I said.

I turned back to him. "I could see it. In your eyes. How scared you are. You've got the kind of eyes that don't hide anything," he said.

I felt my face getting red. But then it made me smile. Partly 'cause I just feel this soul connection with EZ and sometimes we just say the same things. I always looked at a person's eyes. I just wished I could find answers that would solve my confusion.

"People used to say I had eyes like that," he said softly. "But I learned how to work them. To hide stuff."

"You think that's better?"

A tall skinny boy turned the corner, giving us a look as he passed. EZ stared back and the guy kind of waved and kept walking.

"I don't know what's better," EZ said. "What's gonna happen is gonna happen. You feel like walking? Getting out of here for a bit?"

"What's the penalty for cutting?" I asked, even though I knew I could lose Sadie if EZ and I became close again. But I swear, at that moment I didn't care what happened, I would follow him anywhere. He was what I wanted, and I was tired of taking people because they wanted me. Not that I didn't want Sadie as a friend, but she made the first move when I was lovestruck over EZ.

I was just savoring the moment, like I did when I ate my mother's *pasteles* at Christmas time. This was the one place I'd wanted to be for such a long time.

Ezekiel smiled. "I don't know. Never been caught."

"Me either," I said, laughing and appreciating his

rebelliousness. I also knew if his mom caught him, she would whip his butt.

He lifted his backpack onto his shoulder. "Which class will you miss?"

"History with Mr. Leash. We're learning about the amendments to the Constitution."

"Great. Tell him you practiced your 'freedom to assemble' with your homeboy tomorrow. 'Sides, Sadie's in that class. She'll give you the four-one-one. I'll ask her tonight."

"No!" I blurted. "Sadie might not understand us cutting and all. We had this whole conversation about cutting, and she said that she thought it wasn't cool, I don't want to ruin how she thinks of me."

"Who cares? It's only Sadie. She stresses about everything, she's too intense. And when did you start caring what people think, Ms. Rebel?"

"I like our friendship. And I'm mad excited about the group we're putting together for the talent show. I haven't been this happy since I started at this freakin' school. I just don't want to mess it up. Not a word to your sister."

He shrugged his shoulders. "Whatever you say."

"Promise. I know how you be teasing her," I said.

"Promise."

"Now cross your heart."

"I cross my heart," he said as he went through the crossing motions. "There. Make you happy?"

"You wanna go hang out in Stern Grove?"

I nodded and bent over to tie the laces on my new red PUMA sneakers. "Sure."

"Then I'm following you," he said.

It had rained all morning but now the sun was out again, warm and bright. Ezekiel pulled off his jacket and stuffed it across his backpack straps so that it hung down behind him. We crossed Nineteenth Avenue and headed into Stern Grove. I could smell the eucalyptus leaves everywhere and remembered coming here for a Tito Puente concert in the park with my father when I was little.

Two older Black women, holding hands and looking in love, smiled at us.

Ezekiel smiled back and chuckled.

"What's that for?" I asked.

"I'm used to White people frowning at me when I'm with Jessica because she's White. It felt good to get that nod of approval. They always ask her if she's all right, 'cause she's with me," he said. He looked happy and at peace.

I moved closer to him. "That's 'cause most of the people in this area are just sheltered rich people," I said. "I get stared at all the time, no matter who I'm with or where I go. And it bugs me that I just can't be left in peace."

"Yeah, but you're not a Black male with dreadlocks."

"Well, FYI, Black and Latina women are also filling up the prisons at a mad clip, so it ain't all about you, my brotha," I said.

Ezekiel looked at me for a moment, then looked away. I could see his jawbone moving beneath his skin. He knew what I knew. "So why they gotta stare at us for being Black and Hispanics?" he said.

"Latinos," I said. "And they stare because they can."

"So, how do we make 'em stop?"

And for some reason I didn't have an answer and that really bothered me. We walked for a while without saying anything. I felt hot. Why don't people just speak out? Usually I would have come up with some saying or piece of wisdom that was ground into me by my father. But I was paralyzed and tired. I just shut down and didn't want to deal. Too much had happened lately, and I was tired.

I still hadn't come to terms with what happened between Sadie and me two weeks ago. Maybe those lesbians were smiling at us 'cause they saw right through me and knew I was gay too. Sadie picked me out of the lunchroom that first day of school. Maybe the entire world knew what I couldn't seem to figure out. Is everyone either totally gay or totally straight? Can I have feelings for Sadie and maybe never ever be into another girl again? Does this make me gay? Bisexual? A freak? Where do folks go who just have a bunch of questions and no answers?

"If my mom knew I cut school, she'd hit the roof," said

Ezekiel. "She'd lecture me about how she and my dad worked hard so my sister and I could go to school and not have to work like they did in high school."

"Do your parents complain about the opportunities you have that they didn't?" I asked, my voice coming slowly and shakily. We were walking along a cobblestone path, and I tried to let the older women slip from my mind.

EZ glanced at me, then looked away and shook his head. "My dad doesn't say much as long as he knows I go to school every day and get good grades. Other than that, he's always working and I never really see him. Whatever."

"That's too bad, right?"

He shrugged. "It's whatever. What about your dad?"

"He used to be cool."

"You like him?" he asked.

"Sometimes," I said, really not wanting to ruin the moment. "Here is good," I said, stopping at a wide patch of grass underneath a eucalyptus tree overlooking the amphitheater where all the free concerts are held on Sundays. The air around us was thick, hot and stifling. I didn't feel the usual ocean breeze. When I looked at EZ he was still frowning.

"Yeah," EZ said. "This is cool. You want to sit on my jacket?"

I shook my head no and spread my own jacket beneath me, suddenly afraid to be too close to him.

Ezekiel sat down next to me, so close I could see the tiny hairs growing above his top lip. They were very black—like his hair—and fine. It felt strange having him so close to me.

"I never thought he'd leave. My father that is," I said. "I don't think I care so much anymore. There's a part of me that doesn't believe anyone's ever going to stay. Anywhere."

"Do you wonder if he'll ever come back?"

I looked up at the leaves and squinted, liking the way the green twisted and blurred in the sunlight. I felt lighter somehow. Free. "Squint like this, EZ. And see what it does to the leaves."

EZ looked up and squinted, then smiled. "Feels like I'm spinning," he said. "Or like the whole world is spinning and I'm the only thing on it that's not moving."

I felt his hand closing over mine and swallowed. It felt warm and soft and good. I also felt like this must be a dream. Was this really happening?

I closed my eyes, wanting to stay this way always, with the sun warm against my face and EZ's hand on mine. I became a little startled as I heard something shuffling in the bushes.

"Did you hear that?"

"It's probably a bunch of squirrels chasing after each other."

"No, it sounded like footsteps."

"You're just paranoid we're gonna get caught for cutting."

"Yeah, maybe that's it." Trying to be open and not ruin this special moment with defensiveness.

"You ever wish you were small again, Mariposa? That there was someone tucking you in and reading you stories?"

I turned my hand over and laced my fingers in his. His hand was soft and warm. Above us, the leaves fluttered, strips of sun streaming gold down through them. "All the time," I whispered.

"Me too. You gonna let me kiss you, Mariposa?"

I nodded, feeling my stomach rise and dip, rise and dip, until EZ's lips were on mine, soft and warm as his hand.

Our lips slowly separated. I looked toward the amphitheater. "I'm gonna perform one day on that stage, EZ. But right now the only place I want to be is here with you."

CHAPTER 13

AFTERMATH

I was both excited and freaked out about going back to school. Last night I dreamed of kissing Ezekiel's full soft lips. It was beautiful, and it allowed me to sleep soundly. Then Sadie appeared in the dream, told him everything that happened between her and me. Ezekiel was furious and never wanted to speak to me again.

He said, "You don't mess with family like that, Mariposa." Sadie just stood there and smiled and I felt so small.

I regretted what had happened between Sadie and me; it soured my happy moment with EZ with guilt. I was acting like Liza, selling out my friends for some guy.

She and I really hadn't spoken since Sadie's sleepover. It didn't even cross my mind until she missed Spanish class Monday and today. She's probably just mad at me, I thought. But it wasn't like her to not call. First Liza, now Sadie. I liked the idea of having someone to lunch with once

Sadie and I started to become homegirls. Now it's back to being a loner without a crew.

On my way to history class, I passed Evita and Sadie as they walked to class. Evita gave me the evil eye, like she was putting some kind of *brujeria* on me that would keep me away from Sadie. Normally, I would have given it back, but something told me she knew what had happened between Sadie and me, so I sucked in her anger because I felt I deserved it.

I entered class ready to pretend that everything was fine. I tried to pay attention to Mr. Leash as he talked about the Constitution that he so loved.

"So, Ms. Matthews, what do you think about the First Amendment and the separation of church and state?"

"Well, I believe that religion is a personal thing. And one's faith should not be shoved down the throat of another, especially when religious beliefs are used to condemn someone for their sexual preference. Personally, I don't want to pray to any God that would be that judgmental. Race is finally protected—even gender—under the Constitution. So isn't it about time we dealt with gay marriage?" said Sadie.

"I'm cool with watching Angelina Jolie and Eva Mendes make out. But two dudes? That would be gross. It isn't natural," yelled Rio from the back of the room.

"He wasn't talking to you anyway," said Sadie.

"He's entitled to his opinion, Ms. Matthews. Just

answer me this. If the church is so bad, then why are you supporting the caravan that your mother's church is organizing?"

"Yeah, if you believe in this separation between church and state, then that clothes drive you're doing shouldn't be happening at this school," said Rio.

"Just shut up, Rio. You have a point, Mr. Leash. And I'm helping my mom do this 'cause no one else in this school wanted to organize a thing to help with Katrina victims. But that still doesn't excuse Rio from making homophobic comments that make other people feel unsafe."

Mr. Leash walked toward Sadie and towered over her. "You're entitled to your opinion, but in my class we play by my rules."

"Which really means, my opinion only matters if I agree with you, right?"

"So, let's talk about gay marriage to make Ms. Matthews happy," said Mr. Leash.

And, of course, everyone in the class laughed, making Sadie even more angry. I knew I should probably speak up, but I wasn't ready to take on this discussion.

"I'd become a lesbian if I could do it with Sadie and Mariposa," said Rio.

"Shut up, you freakin' crankhead," said Sadie.

The class laughed hysterically. And I wanted to be anywhere but in this classroom. I know he said that because Liza must have told him that Sadie and I kissed.

Mr. Leash just walked to the chalkboard and began writing the questions for our quiz, proving that his own ideas about how the amendments should be interpreted didn't agree with Sadie's opinions and turning his back to the blatant homophobia.

But Rio couldn't leave well enough alone. "I'm surprised Liza's straight after being Mariposa's friend."

"Shut up, Rio, " I said. "You're going too far."

Now he crossed the line. I lunged across a row of desks and went straight for his throat. I don't know what came over me, but I just saw red and all I wanted to do was beat the mess out of Rio. And after I was finished with him I wanted to find Liza and rip her a new one. It's one thing if she wants to mess up her own life, but now she's interfering in mine.

Mr. Leash was on the phone to the assistant principal by the time I had Rio in a choke hold. Rio became like a scared child. "I was just playing. I didn't mean anything by it," said Rio.

"Take it back, asshole." But he didn't, so I tightened my choke hold even more.

"All right, I take it back," said Rio, barely able to speak.

"Sadie and I are just friends. Nothing more." I looked at Sadie as I spoke, hoping that maybe by defending our honor things would be squashed between us. Instead, she just turned away and pretended to be more interested in looking at the girls playing soccer outside.

Assistant principal Mrs. Hillaire entered in a panic. Mr. Leash pointed to me. "She's the instigator, take her to the office."

Mrs. Hillaire pulled me off the ground and once Rio was able to regain his footing, he yelled, "You outed yourself, Mariposa. I didn't have to say a word!"

Mr. Leash put his finger to his lips motioning for Rio to be quiet. "If you don't stop this nonsense, Mr. Lopez, you can join her." Rio patted down his ruffled hair and then took his seat.

I realized he was right. Letting him get to me made everything seem like it was true. My temper got the best of me and I incriminated us both. Sometimes I acted without thinking. Sadie is more calculating about her outbursts. That's why I'm going to get suspended and go home. Next time, I'll remember to keep my mouth shut.

CHAPTER 14

IT ALL COMES TUMBLING DOWN

A week passed since the homophobic incident in history class. After it all was said and done, I was suspended for a week. And suddenly everything around me felt cold. I really regretted what had happened between Sadie and me. But at the same time it hurt that she hadn't even called to see how I was after I got kicked out of class. At least Liza called to make sure she and I were cool. Don't get me wrong, I read her the riot act, but eventually I came around to forgiving her. It's hard to stay mad at Liza. She's like the sister I never wanted.

I guess when your friend's involved you just gotta understand that whatever you tell her she will share with her boyfriend. Normally, it wouldn't have been a problem because I keep my business to myself. This time though, I had to share 'cause it felt like I had nowhere else to turn.

Once Liza and I were cool, she said, "You and Sadie gotta make up. We got to get our stuff together and win the talent show."

"Since when are you all into this talent show thing?"

"I've missed us doing our thing. And I want my friend back."

"You weren't checkin' for me last week," I said.

"Well, that was because I thought you had Sadie and didn't need me anymore."

"You wouldn't have felt replaced if you hadn't dumped me for some dude in the first place."

"I just knew you would understand."

"Yeah, I do. But when I like someone, I don't dump my friends. And now it's gonna be even harder for Rio and me to be cool."

"I'm gonna tell you like I told him. Give it time," said Liza.

I did think it was odd that Liza was suddenly all concerned about the talent show and making sure the Sista Hood won. Personally, I hadn't touched my sketchbook all week, and the talent show was the last thing on my mind. Normally, I would be drowning my sadness in my lyrics, but for some reason I didn't feel inspired. I just wanted to waste away watching *Brown Sugar*—my guilty pleasure movie that I discovered at the video store this summer. It reminded me of Ezekiel and me. I just kept hoping that it didn't take us as long to finally get together as it did Taye Diggs and Sanaa Lathan.

I was sitting in my living room wearing a T-shirt and boxers, watching the end of *Brown Sugar* when they finally get together, when the phone rang. My mother rushed to answer it.

"Mariposa, it's one of your friends."

Mom picked up the phone and handed it to me. Frankly, I was too interested in my movie to care who it was.

I started coughing and gave my mom the sweetest look I could conjure up. In my lowest voice, practically lip-synching the words, I said, "I'm not well, you answer it."

Obviously, Mom wasn't buying me being sick. "Mariposa take this phone call now. You're going to go crazy if you keep yourself all locked up in this house in front of the television."

Then she pushed the phone at me. And I dropped it like it was on fire. It crashed to the floor and all I could hear was Sadie yelling, "Hello!"

I picked up the phone.

"Hello," I said, coughing.

"Hello. It's me."

"Umm, hey, what's up?"

"I'm good, how are you?"

"Sick," I said.

Then I coughed again, but louder. My mother just stood there nodding her head in disapproval. I waved my arms toward the bedroom. My mom disappeared into her room with a full glass of wine.

"Sadie, shit, I mean fuck, I mean—how are you?"

Once again I had managed to make a complete fool of myself. I started to cough again to make my sickness more believable. I stopped coughing, and there was just this awkward silence. I didn't know what to say. But more than anything, I didn't want to hurt her feelings.

"Hey, we need to talk," said Sadie.

"Sorry if I've seemed a bit distant. It's just I've been sick and my mom has been a little crazed over the divorce." I wasn't lying, I was sick with the Matthews love virus.

"I've been thinking a lot about what happened," said Sadie.

I knew she was feeling me out, hoping I would reveal how I felt first. I admit, I liked how I felt when we kissed, but I don't know if I could really be with a girl. But Sadie is so special and no matter what, I didn't want to lose her friendship.

My dad always said, "Your friends are in your life either for a reason, a season or a lifetime." I want Sadie to be one of those lifetime friends. I can be myself around her.

"What happened was really special," I said.

I meant what I said. Had it been anyone else, I wouldn't have been as open.

"Thanks for sticking up for me in class," said Sadie.

"He had it coming. And I should have spoken up earlier."

"For real. I just shut down when Mr. Leash mentioned my mother," said Sadie. "I don't know what I would do if she ever found out that I was gay. How is everything with your mother?"

"We haven't spoken about us kissing. Either she doesn't want to deal with it or was too drunk to remember."

"I don't know who's worse, your mother or mine," said Sadie. "I feel bad you got suspended 'cause I was afraid to stick up for you."

"I was a jerk after we kissed. And if we're making apologies, then I have something to tell you."

I kept reminding myself that the truth will set you free, but I felt like what I was about to reveal to Sadie could end our friendship forever. "I kissed your brother the other day in Stern Grove."

"I know, I saw you. But I'm glad you told me," said Sadie. "Do you care about him as much as he does about you?"

"I've been in love with him since we met this summer. Wait. How do you know he cares about me?"

"I was walking through the park with Evita that day and she noticed the two of you."

"But we were cutting school."

"Yeah? So were we."

"But you never cut. And why didn't you say anything?" I asked.

"And ruin such a bittersweet moment? Hell no! Well, if you didn't want anyone to see, you should have kissed under a tree and not in the center of an open amphitheater."

"I wasn't planning for it to happen, it just did," I said.

I started to feel less open and wanted to hang up the phone before things worsened and I became sick for real. But now I was worried about whether or not EZ knew about Sadie and me.

"Does he know about us?" I asked.

"I came out to EZ, Mariposa, and then I came clean about you and me."

"What? There was only a kiss, there is no you and me!" I said, afraid to know how EZ reacted.

"Well, I wasn't kissing myself."

"True, but I was confused," I said.

I wanted to run to EZ, to make sure everything was fine. Now I knew why he hadn't called since our kiss.

"Was he mad?" I said.

"He said he needed some time to figure things out.

The rest he'll have to tell you himself," said Sadie. "I'm willing to forgive and forget, if you are?"

"Yeah. It's all cool," I said.

Then came this moment of relief, like, finally Sadie and I might be okay after all.

"Let's just try not to have any more secrets. Be honest," said Sadie.

"I agree."

"So was I your first kiss?" said Sadie.

"Excuse me?" I said.

"Well?"

"No," I said. I thought about telling her that I had kissed a girl before but I didn't.

"Okay."

I felt that tingle all over that you get when you're embarrassed, like a quick electric shock that comes from your stomach. But I didn't feel paralyzed anymore. I could speak.

"Was I your first kiss?" I asked, pretending not to care much about the answer.

"Yes," she said, laughing, a little nervously. "My first kiss with a girl."

"Oh," I said, genuinely surprised.

Sadie laughed. I liked adding a little shock value to the conversation and putting Sadie on the spot. She never seemed to lose her cool.

"Have you ever kissed a dude?" I asked.

"Yeah."

"Do you like it better with a dude or a girl?"

"It feels more natural with a girl. It just feels right."

"So how was it with me?"

"You were a'ight, when you relaxed."

"I was just a'ight?"

"Honestly, I thought you could have been better."

"I guess game runs in the Matthews family. Do I hear a mack in the making?"

"A mack? I wish. If I had half the game my brother did, I would always be happy."

I'm a little hurt that Sadie thought my kisses were only average. After everything that went down, I honestly thought she was a good kisser. To be honest, I enjoyed kissing them both. I do find Sadie attractive, but dealing with the stares and all the hard stuff that comes with being gay, it felt like too much now. Plus, I needed her to be in my life for the long haul and from everything I've learned about love, I know it doesn't last forever. Then I started to have visions of being twenty and alone. So I just thought, screw it. I took a deep breath and spoke my truth. "Honestly, I really enjoyed it," I said.

But then I thought about having a husband and kids one day, and I got scared. Curiosity is one thing. But being in a relationship with a girl is something I'm not ready for. I just felt safe with Sadie. It felt right in the moment. Does that make me gay?

There. It felt like a massive boulder had been taken off my shoulders.

"You're not the only one. Confused, I mean," said Sadie.

"What do you mean, you're confused? I thought you knew what you wanted," I asked.

"I'm not confused about being a lesbian. I'm confused about who I like."

"Now I'm really confused." For some reason I knew I really didn't want to hear what Sadie was about to tell me. I wanted to feel adored. I needed to feel special. I wanted to be her best kiss ever. I guess that's not fair, but I'm just being real. Sadie is supposed to be the solid one, the one who is predictable and always the voice of reason. I asked, "So, there's someone besides me?"

"If we're gonna be girls, then I have to come clean. There's someone else. And it wasn't until you left that I realized you and I weren't it."

She's gonna dump me over a kiss. Great. Maybe I should just stay away from the Matthews family.

"I really thought you would turn my world around. But when I kissed Evita for the first time at Stern Grove, it was magical."

"Evita!" I yelled. "You like Evita? Then why did you even mess with me?"

"Evita and I never slept together or kissed each other. We were just close friends. Then she started hanging out with Bethany Doll and I started to feel jealous. I wanted more, but it was too late. I feared my mom and what she would do if she ever found out. Then I saw you the first day of school and forgot all about my feelings for her. I even wanted to kiss you twice to make sure."

"I get it, I'm your experiment. Well, I feel used."

"I'm sorry, Mariposa. I feel so close to you and I don't want to lose your friendship. I just had to be honest. It's all that Christian guilt my mother has drilled into me."

As much as I wanted to be mad at Sadie, I couldn't. Because what really bugged me the most was that Evita was a better kisser than me. How could she be better than me? She's always freakin' better than me. And I was tired of being second best.

"Was I at least okay?" I asked, sounding pathetic.

"You sound jealous. I thought you were confused and didn't know if this was the time for you to be with me anyways."

"Yeah, but I still have my ego."

"I've liked girls since I was seven," said Sadie.

"Really?"

"I had this fat crush on my next-door neighbor. We played house and doctor all the time. Then she moved away and broke my heart."

"Ay, *bendita*," I said with no real sympathy.

"Smart-ass. But for real though, it's not easy. How many Black lesbians have you ever seen? And my mom being religious and all? It was scary to be me as a little girl. I used to pray to God to make me straight. Then I would go to sleep and dream about Destiny's Child. It was useless."

"Destiny's Child!? You think they're fine? What about Goapele or Mystic? Now, they're fine. If Mystic was gay, I think I could be with her," I said.

"Now, Beyoncé she's fine. I love how sexy and voluptuous she is. Mystic and Goapele are too skinny."

"But they're fine. Anyone can lose or gain weight. But if you ugly, ain't nothing you can do about it," I said.

"Whatever, Mariposa! If you were telling me that you were into their powerful words and respected their minds, I could give you that, but you're just being superficial."

I knew Sadie had a point. But male or female, I wasn't gonna kiss ugly. I'm all about da sistahood, but it's one thing to be friends and another to get your freak on. It's not like Mystic or Goapele are hoochies. They don't wear extensions and you never read about their love lives in gossip magazines.

"Hey, how was EZ about you being a lesbian?"

"He wasn't surprised. Claimed he always knew."

"Kinda easy when his clothes are always missing," I said.

"He said he loved me no matter what. And he didn't really believe any of my mother's Bible garbage anyhow."

"So, we're cool. I mean, friends?"

"Totally fine," said Sadie.

"See you later for rehearsal," I said.

"See you then," she said, with a distance that made it seem like we were oceans apart.

We hung up the phone. And for some reason I felt both relieved and dissed. Maybe I was still confused about being gay. Or maybe I felt weird about getting dumped before we were ever a couple. Honestly, I just worried that no one would ever love me like my Papi once loved my Mami.

CHAPTER 15

INSPIRATION

I opened my sketchbook for the first time in a week to my list: *the ten things I must do to win Ezekiel's love.* I wanted to crumble it up and throw it in the trash, but I wasn't ready to let it go yet. Instead, I turned the page to a clean sheet of paper and began my new list: <u>the ten steps toward creating a sistahood</u>, by Mariposa Colón. I took out my markers and colored in each letter. Underneath, in my best graffiti, I wrote:

1. Find something you can all share, like hip-hop, going to an all-White school, etc.
2. Support one another in becoming better people.
3. Tell the truth, even when it's hard.
4. Don't fall in love with each other or their family members. It's too much drama.

5. Never sacrifice the sistahood for your new heart-throb.

6. Be open to new ideas, you're not the only brilliant one.

7. Remember the sistahood is the family you create, so be selective.

8. Conflict is bound to happen, so don't be afraid of it.

9. If someone in the sistahood has a boyfriend or girlfriend, assume anything you tell them will be shared.

10. Don't always be hard, let them know you care.

I then made three copies of the list for each of the girls, which I planned to give to them at our next rehearsal. Maybe they could each add to the list or the list could change over the years, depending upon what each of us needed. I then ripped my list out and posted it on my wall above my desk as a reminder of how important the sistahood has become to me.

I felt inspired to finally write our song for the talent show. The chorus came to me first:

The options are there, if you choose to care,
Just believe in yourself and you're almost there.

I decided to take a break and walked over to my mother's room to watch television.

"Can you es-plain this to me, Mariposa?" she asked, handing me a white card from the school with one hand and holding a glass of wine in the other.

"Explain what?" It was Saturday evening. Instead of running the streets like most kids my age I was sitting at home writing rhymes. My mother was sitting at the table, tipsy, dangling a white card between her thumb and forefinger as though it were something dirty.

"This absence." She held the card up and read in her broken English: "Dear Parent. Please be in-form-ed that your child was ab-sent from her his-tory class on Thursday, February twenty-second."

I shrugged. February 22. Last week. The first time EZ and I kissed. "I didn't go. What's there to explain?"

"*Pero* you went to school, *qué no?*"

I didn't want to have to explain anything to her while she was drinking. She becomes a different person. Cold, distant and she doesn't listen.

"Mariposa," said Mom, "I'm talking to you."

"Of course, I went to school that day. I just didn't go to history class."

"*Por favor*, Mariposa, don't do this. Don't do this to me after all that I've been through with your Papi. I don't need this. First you miss your class and then you get kicked from school for fighting a boy."

"I didn't need you to shut Dad out and make him leave."

"It's his fault, don't blame me."

I glared at her.

"I wondered when you would get angry at me," she said. "You got angry with your dad, but never me." She held up the card. "So, I guess this is anger then, no?"

"You don't know anything, Mom. History class has nothing to do with you. Believe it or not, everything is not always about you."

"I know a lot of things." She turned to leave, then stopped. "Maybe you think you have all the answers right now because of your new friends, but you don't."

"I have to study Spanish. Remember, the class I'm failing?"

"You'll see how life plays tricks on you," she said.

I stared out the window for a long time after she left. The sky was overcast and gray. My Mami was right. My life was already playing tricks on me. And all I wanted was to be a little girl again, so that my papi could tuck me into bed and tell me that everything was going to be fine.

CHAPTER 16

THE REHEARSAL

I walked around the block three times trying to get up the courage to walk into Sadie's house. I had faced Sadie, but talking with EZ wasn't as easy. After all, he knew about Sadie and me. When I finally gathered the courage to step off the curve, a car almost hit me. Great, just my luck. I leaped back and caught my breathe. I wasn't ready to face Ezekiel and what did I get myself into, getting with his sister? Drama. You don't mess with family. And you really don't mess with men who are already involved.

I shielded my eyes from the sun and prepared to enter. I had to suck up my pride for the Sista Hood. After all, what was most important is that we win the talent show. Priorities, Mariposa. Then, before I could cross the street,

Jessica and Ezekiel pulled up in front of Ezekiel's house and he leaned over to kiss her for what seemed like an eternity. I just watched, not caring if they noticed me staring. They broke their lip-lock as I sauntered past her car. EZ noticed me, smiled and then went down for another kiss. Forget you, I thought as I walked up the Matthews's front stairs. No, stupid me for ever thinking you were worth my time.

My Papi, EZ, Rio—dudes are all the same. Papi never told me that as he was preparing his little girl to be a warrior. He always told me I could do whatever a boy could do. He wanted me to do well in school and eventually go to college. But not once did he ever tell me that I would be hurt because most men weren't prepared to deal with a strong, intelligent, stubborn young sistah like me. It's never enough. Yeah, Papi loved me, but it was a whole different story for his own relationships with women. I get it now. Fine.

I knocked on the door as Ezekiel ran to the door and J-Ho drove off. He pulled out his keys and I just stood there waiting for what seemed like an eternity for the door to open. As he fiddled with his keys, his arm brushed against mine. His touch made me shiver, and to be honest, I just wished he would kiss me right there in front of the entire neighborhood. Proudly, I held it together. I wasn't going to be the first to break the silence.

Ezekiel turned to me. "Mari, I only kissed her to

make you jealous. I've been trying to call you all week and you never answered my calls. I really wanted to talk about what happened. Then when Sadie told me what happened between the two of you, I figured that maybe you really wanted to be with her. I wouldn't want you and I together to break Sadie's heart."

Just as I was about to respond, Mrs. Matthews opened the door and welcomed me into the house. "Oh, Mari, it's wonderful to see you again. The girls are waiting for you upstairs."

"Thank you, Mrs. Matthews," I said.

Then Mrs. Matthews glared at Ezekiel. "Did you break it off with that tramp yet? Why couldn't you be with a good girl like Mariposa."

He looked at me with this "I wish we could talk" look. But I backed down and just rushed up the stairs. I was tired of being hurt, and I began to feel that maybe I was better off alone. Once I got to the top of the stairs I couldn't help but eavesdrop.

"She's not a tramp, Mama. And stop trying to control my life. I'm not a little boy anymore."

"Well, you got to act like a man to be treated like one."

"Nothing is ever good enough for you. Why can't you just love me unconditionally?"

"Young man, I don't know what's got into you, but if you don't stop I'm going to slap the devil out of you."

"I'll save you the energy. I'm leaving. Later."

And Ezekiel just walked out the door like he was never gonna return. Mrs. Matthews was speechless. Ezekiel had never spoken back to his mother.

I slipped into Sadie's room as Mrs. Matthews began to ascend the stairs. And just when I thought things could never get any worse, I entered to see Evita and Sadie lip-locked in a kiss on Sadie's bed. They were startled to see me but knowing that Mrs. Matthews was only a few paces behind me, I rushed to the pillows on the bed and began a pillow fight with the girls. The girls just sat there, confused by my actions.

"Freakin' pick up a pillow and start fighting with me 'cause your mom is right behind me."

They sat there frozen.

"Did you hear me? Now!"

I picked up a pillow and started wailing Evita with it. It kinda felt good. Then Sadie joined me just as Mrs. Matthews opened the door to us laughing, playing and having fun as all good girls do.

"See, why can't your brother be like my Sadie, a good child that never talks back."

And we all just stood there smiling and acting all saintlike until she shut the door.

"What happened?" Sadie asked.

"Your mom was talking all bad about J-Ho and your brother spoke back to her."

"For real?" Sadie said.

Evita chimed in with her two cents. "Ezekiel is always so respectful to your mom. I mean, we all are. She just demands respect."

"Well, not only did he talk back, he left the house too."

"That's not like Ezekiel," said Sadie. "Something else must be going on with him."

"In the eight weeks I knew EZ at camp, he never once lost his temper. He's one of the most mellow guys I know."

"I feel bad about busting him and Jessica out. But that was before I came out to him. That's why my mom is on his case. I never thought he could be so understanding. Most of the time he's just self-absorbed," said Sadie.

"Yeah, one time I went to use the bathroom, and EZ was just standing in front of the mirror plucking his eyebrows," Evita said. "Then he turned to me and asked if he should wax them. I was like, dude, you have no hair? He swore me to secrecy and then shut the door."

"From then on Evita and I held it over his head every time he was mean to us," said Sadie.

"Really?" I couldn't believe that EZ spent that much time worrying about himself. He looked so naturally gorgeous, I always thought it was all effortless for him. "I guess dudes are insecure too."

Before I could walk over to Sadie to comfort her, Evita scooted in toward Sadie and put her hand on her back. "It'll be okay, Sadie."

Sadie just sat on the bed trying to hold back the tears.

"It's just that I'm tired of pretending to be something I'm not. I wish I could be gutsy like my brother."

"It's all right, *amorcita*, we do what we can when we can. Look how afraid I am with my own parents. My dad would kill me if he knew I was gay. I even pushed you away and hung out with Bethany trying to pretend I was something I wasn't while you have always been Sadie, and I love who you are," said Evita.

I tried to let Evita take the lead with Sadie. And I was doing well until I put my foot in my mouth. "Yeah, at least you never pretended to be White."

But Evita was so into Sadie, and vice versa, they didn't even know I was there.

"How about we start practicing for the tryouts and get our minds off all this stress?" I said.

Sadie jumped up, glad to get her mind off her problems.

"Where's Liza?" said Sadie.

"Late as usual, of course," said Evita.

And though I knew Evita was right, Liza was still my homegirl, and whatever I had to say to her would be done face-to-face. "She has some things going on today," I lied.

I did find it strange that Liza didn't even call to say she would be late. She'd been gone so much lately. I gotta check in with her and find out what's going on for real, I thought.

"Her problem is that creepy boyfriend of hers," said Evita.

"Dudes are just difficult. Complex in their simplicity, as my mother claims," said Sadie.

I wished I could say something nice about Rio, but Evita was right about him being creepy. It was getting to the point that I was worried about Liza. Then I again had to witness Evita and Sadie locking lips while my own love life was going nowhere.

"A'ight, lovebirds, can you at least wait till I leave," I said.

They pulled away. "Sorry," said Sadie.

"Yeah, sorry," said Evita with a big smile.

"Cool. Can we practice now?"

"Sure," they both said like scolded children.

"But first, Mari, I have something to say," said Evita.

I got a little nervous, thinking we might have one of those lesbian processing sessions. Where we talk, cry, talk some more and then cry a lot more. Emotionally, I just wasn't in the space. But I was happy to see that at least one couple in my life seemed stable.

"I just want to say that I'm sorry I've been so mean to you. Since the first day of school, I was jealous of you, 'cause my girl over here couldn't talk about anyone else. She was crushed out on you. And I was all wrong about you. You're really good people. Do you think we could start over?"

Part of me was like, heck no. But after Evita defended me in Spanish class and helped me pass my midterms, I knew she was good people too.

"Yeah, sure. Everyone deserves a second chance. And if Sadie cares about you enough to want to be your *novia*, then you must be *buena gente*."

I gave her a hug, and I really meant it. But seeing Sadie smile with joy that her girls made peace was the best reward.

I pulled out the scribbles I had been working on for our show song and read them the chorus. "It's a work-in-progress. Maybe we can work out the kinks at practice today."

This rehearsal would have been perfect if Liza was there. "I was gonna give you each a copy of this top ten list I wrote for the Sista Hood last night, but I want to wait till Liza is with us."

"Why don't we start practice, I'm sure Liza will walk in at any moment," said Evita.

We were about to start practice when my cell rang. I picked it up and answered, "Hello."

"Mariposa, it's Liza. I need you to come get me. It's an emergency."

Liza was full of drama, but she had never called me saying it was an emergency, and she never called me sounding like she did then on the phone.

"Sure, I'll be right there." I grabbed my sketchbook from my backpack and scribbled down the address. "Don't worry, it will all be okay."

CHAPTER 17

DÓNDE ESTÁ LIZA?

I entered the emergency room of San Francisco's General Hospital with Sadie, Evita and Mrs. Matthews. Mrs. Matthews demanded that she come too to make sure that everything would be fine. And as we all knew, winning an argument with Mrs. Matthews was never gonna happen. In the final hour, I was grateful that she was with us as she knew exactly how to tread through the red tape.

She walked up to the emergency room registration clerk. "Can you please direct me to Liza Ortiz? She's a patient here."

"If you can please take a seat, I'll be with you in a moment," said the clerk.

Everything about the emergency room was chaotic.

Children were crying. A gentleman was throwing up in the corner. A pregnant woman was screaming bloody murder as her contractions got worse and she was carted away on a gurney. A couple sat there fighting about how much this visit would cost them. Sirens rang loudly as an ambulance pulled up to the hospital with a stabbed kid who was bleeding all over. And, of course, there were only two seats left, one of which we gave to Mrs. Matthews as we waited.

The triage nurse finally called Mrs. Matthews over and I went with her. "We've been trying to contact Liza's mother, but we can't seem to get through. Do you know of another number?"

"No. I've just gotten to know Liza. She's friends with my daughter, Sadie. How about you let us in and then we'll work on getting her mother here. Her best friend, Mariposa, wants to make sure she's okay."

"That's fine. Maybe Mariposa can help me figure out what happened."

I agreed, nodding my head. She then lead us to Liza's room. We motioned for Evita and Sadie to join us as we followed the nurse. When we entered, Liza was rolled in a ball like a scared kitten. I wasn't used to seeing Liza look so weak. She was always such a tomboy, full of energy and life. Her back was to us, so I couldn't see her face. I walked to the other side so I could see. Her face looked like someone had taken sandpaper to half of it as her skin was raw and bruised.

I'm not gonna front, I flinched and jumped when I saw how bad she looked. "Liza, we're here. Are you okay?"

As soon as Liza heard my voice, she lifted herself up and into my arms with whatever strength she had left. And she just cried, and said, "I'm so sorry." She just kept repeating those three words over and over.

"It's not your fault, Liza. We're here and you're going to be fine."

I started to cry and at that very moment I swear I wished I had killed Rio while I had the chance. Once we were able to calm Liza down, the nurse motioned for me to ask her questions.

"What happened, Liza?"

Liza looked around to see who was in the room as if she was protecting someone. "I'm only gonna talk if the nurse leaves." But the nurse just stood there.

"I think we'll be fine here," Mrs. Matthews told the nurse, giving her a little wink. Once she was given the Matthews step-to-the-curb command, the nurse left us to deal with Liza alone.

"Okay, Liza, what happened?" I asked.

Liza started crying, not even tripping over Mrs. Matthews being in the room. "I don't want you to hate me."

"I could never hate you, *chica*. You're my homegirl," I said.

"Rio and I had gone to Dolores Park to check out this dealer that supplies him with, you know . . ."

"Drugs?"

"Yeah. Rio had gone a full twenty-four hours without getting high, he was bored out of his drug-free mind. So he decided to try the hard stuff."

"And what happened to you?"

"Well, whatever his hookup gave him was laced with some crazy stuff and Rio just flipped out and started dragging me with my face on the cement up Dolores Street."

"What a loser!"

"It wasn't his fault, Mari. He was on something. I really shouldn't have gotten him mad."

"Don't you get that no matter what you did or said you couldn't have stopped his trip?"

Tears just kept streaming down Liza's face and I knew any criticism of Rio at this moment was pointless. It was most important that Liza felt supported. I sat there just holding her and assuring her that everything would be fine.

"The cops wanted me to press charges and admit that he was on something, but I refused. You can't say anything."

Then Mrs. Matthews put in her two cents. "Well, I didn't promise, and that boy is gonna get his. And you, Liza, need to stay away from him. Once an addict, always an addict."

"Liza, we're all here. Whatever you need, we'll get through this together," I said.

"I just want to see Rio. To tell him it will all be okay."

"What'll be okay, Liza?" I asked.

"That we'll get through this together. All three of us."

It took me a while to realize that Liza was pregnant. That's what had probably set off Rio's frenzy. He can't take care of himself, let alone graduate from high school. How the hell is he going to take care of a child?

"Does the nurse know you're pregnant, Liza?" I asked.

"Yeah, they did a complete examination before you all got here."

Mrs. Matthews hollered for the nurse to come. "Ms. Rappaport, you can come in now."

"You all promised," cried Liza.

"No, Mariposa promised. I, on the other hand, must make sure that you're cared for. We must contact your mother. Is she at work?"

"Yeah."

"Can you remember her number?"

"No."

"Then where's your cell phone, I'm sure the number is in there. Right?"

"You can't tell my mother!"

"Why, Liza?" I said.

Liza sat there shaking and crying more.

"Liza, why can't we tell your mother?" I demanded that she tell me the truth.

"Because my mother left us this summer. And my

brothers are raising me. I'm still underage, if CPS finds out, they'll put me in foster care."

Then Liza just became very still and quiet.

"I'm sorry, Mari. I'm really sorry."

Everything was finally crystal clear. This wasn't the first time that Rio had beaten Liza. The way things were going, it wouldn't be the last. That's why Liza would disappear for weeks at a time, missing school and not showing up when she was supposed to be meeting me. Liza was being battered by that asshole Rio. It all makes so much sense now—his control over her, his possessiveness about her whereabouts, her depression. He probably knew about her mother and was holding that over her head too.

I started to feel like I let her down instead of the other way around. Here I was, all wrapped up in my Matthews love triangle. My parents' divorce, even my mom's drinking had never impacted me to the extent of what was happening to Liza.

All I could do was hug Liza. "No, Liza, I'm sorry that I wasn't a better friend. I should've known."

"But it's okay, 'cause Rio loves me. When everyone left me, he stayed," said Liza.

"We'll talk about it later, Liza. But Sadie's mother is right. You need to stay away from Rio for a while. He's sick, homie. He's real sick."

CHAPTER 18

HEALING

I fell asleep on Liza's bed with her. My resting next to her seemed to be the only thing that calmed her enough to allow her to fall asleep. I awoke to the whispering sounds of her brother, Sadie, Evita and Mrs. Matthews talking about Liza. "Thank you so much for calling me, Mrs. Matthews," said Abraham Ortiz, Liza's older brother. Abraham was still in his uniform from Airborne Express.

"My pleasure," said Mrs. Matthews. Then she handed him a piece of paper with a few numbers scrawled across. "I've worked with her and she's wonderful! I'm positive she'll be able to assist Liza in some way."

"I just hope her tests come back negative," said Abraham."

"I'll be praying to the Lord tonight for the best."

"What tests?" I asked Sadie.

"The doctors wanted to make sure they tested her for

HIV and STDs since she obviously had unprotected sex with a drug user," said Sadie. "I overheard my mother telling her brother."

Like being pregnant wasn't enough for Liza to deal with. Now she has to worry about being sick too.

"I hadn't even thought about that," I said.

"That's why abstinence is the Lord's way," said Mrs. Matthews.

I gave Evita and Sadie the all-knowing look as Mrs. Matthews continued to lecture us about being safe in these last days until Armageddon. And it was in that moment that I really saw just how courageous Sadie was in her love for Evita. I wanted to become a better friend to all my homegirls. To not be so self-absorbed that I'm blind to the world around me. Isn't it ironic that I always thought I was the one that was taking care of everyone and they were draining me? When really, I never listened, I just assumed. I got it now, people aren't there for me because in many ways I'm not really there for them. How many times had I really listened to my friends without thinking about my own problems. Practically never. Of course, they all have their imperfections too. However, I was finally learning to admit my own.

It was there in the hospital as Mrs. Matthews was preparing to drive us all home that I realized why my *Ten things I must do to win Ezekial's love* list never felt right. It was the wrong list. So I opened up my sketchbook and started writing my new list, which was entitled <u>The ten</u> <u>things I must do to become a better friend.</u>

1. Learn to listen.
2. Don't ever assume anything about anyone.
3. Ask more questions.
4. Open my eyes and really see what's up.
5. Trust until proven wrong.
6. It's not always about me.
7. No relationship is better than the wrong relationship.
8. Treat people like you want to be treated.
9. Be honest, don't be afraid to be a truth tella.
10. Always be true to hip-hop by being true to myself.

I'd been spending all my time trying to prove I was worthy of being at Stanford, worthy of Ezekiel loving me, deserving of Sadie's friendship. Proving I was Latina enough. And the entire time, I was enough by just being true to myself. I've always prided myself on honesty, but I was living a lie by what I didn't say. Now I wanted to make it up to the Sista Hood, to Ezekiel and most importantly to myself. I felt complete as I closed my book and resolved to work on my list. I finally felt I was learning to love myself and not expecting someone else to do it for me.

Evita, Sadie and I followed Mrs. Matthews toward

her car. The Romeros, Evita's parents, were waiting for us outside when we exited the hospital. They drove a used minivan, and Evita's seven-year-old sister Sylvia was sleeping in the backseat. Her parents were older than mine, in their mid-sixties. Mr. Romero sat in the driver's seat. While Mrs. Romero got out to greet Mrs. Matthews, Mr. Romero waved to her from his seat.

"Thank you for calling me, Gloria," said Mrs. Romero.

Mrs. Romero's eyes looked as if they had survived many wars. They had dark circles under them and though she seemed very kind, smiling seemed like a huge effort.

"No problem, Betina. Do you mind taking Mariposa home? She lives closer to you."

"No problem."

I got into the car with the Romeros and Mrs. Matthews walked off with Sadie. I was nervous to go. I'd never been alone with Evita. The newness of our getting along still hadn't clicked yet for me. I sat in the very back seat with her. I decided to put my new list into practice through asking questions and not assuming.

"*Gracias*, for taking me home."

Mr. Romero remained silent. He just looked at me through the rearview mirror. He seemed like he could have been a military drill sergeant in another life.

"What part of Nicaragua are you from?" I asked Evita.

"Managua. It's the capital."

"So, why did you leave?"

Everyone in the car grew quiet. Evita just looked at her father and then looked at me.

Mr. Romero opened his mouth for the first time. "The Sandinistas stole our land. We had no choice."

"Who were the Sandinistas?"

"A radical leftist group that overthrew the Somoza government and forced us out of our home," said Mr. Romero.

"Wow, that's horrible. But aren't leftists supposed to be on the side of the people? I only ask because my father considers himself one. He organized with the Young Lords," I said.

"Who were they?" said Evita.

"They were Communists like the Sandinistas, all controlled by the Cubans and the Soviets," said Mr. Romero.

"Actually, they were socialists who were trying to make sure that there was enough water, food and shelter for the poor and working class. And that meant that those who had a lot had to give a little," I said.

"Well, my dad was a general in the Somoza government that tried to save the country against the Sandinistas," Evita said.

"So, basically, your family was rich and had to give up their land so that other people could live."

I guess I said the wrong thing, because Mr. Romero slammed his foot on the brake and both Evita and I jerked forward. He put the car into park, then towered over me, shaking his long hairy finger. Mrs. Romero didn't say a word.

"You. You were born here, entitled to the excess of this country with no clue to what war or sacrifice would ever mean. How dare you tell me my own history. We didn't just lose our land. My parents and my brothers were all killed for this so-called democracy."

I sat there scared that he would attack me. But he didn't. He just finished what he was saying, took a deep breath and then took his position back behind the wheel. We all sat in silence. All I wanted to do was get home as quickly and safely as possible. I should have just asked questions and listened. But, in this case, I think I was right to say what I did. After all, it's okay to have an opinion, right? Maybe he's right, I don't understand. My dad, however, did teach me enough about Latin American history that I don't think I was totally wrong either.

CHAPTER 19

THE RESULTS

The entire Sista Hood went with Liza to the hospital to get her HIV and STD test results. For the first time since I'd known Liza, she actually asked for help and I was happy to support proactively instead of reactively. We went to the Mission Neighborhood Health Center, which is behind the hospital. Liza warned us that Rio would be there, so we were prepared for war. The hospital suggested that Rio be tested too. So today could be the day of reckoning for them both.

We walked into the clinic hoping for the best. Liza signed in at the front desk and the three of us just took a seat. Being at the clinic was so much better than the emergency room. It was a teen clinic so it had posters of famous people encouraging you to get tested. Bright colors were painted on the walls, and free condom and glove jars were placed throughout the office. Sadie and Evita sat there holding hands, which took a lot of guts in such a public space. They were both becoming more fierce about being out.

I had really started to like Evita so much more. She can be mad funny when she stops acting stressed and learns to feel comfortable around you. Yesterday on the phone we were comparing our dads. They had different political views, but they both thought they were right about everything. Evita also confessed to me that her father has cheated on her mother. But when her mother found out, she found herself a lover too, and after that Mr. Romero never cheated again. It surprised me that Mrs. Romero was so independent because when I met her last night she seemed so obedient. But Evita told me that as long as her mother acts like her father is the boss in public, her dad lets her mom do whatever she wants. I gotta give Mrs. Romero mad props for checkin' her man at home.

"Here he comes," said Sadie.

I looked up from my *Seventeen* magazine with nothing but skinny girls plastered over the cover. And there was Rio walking out with his parents from the office. I knew the man with Rio must be Mr. Lopez, his father. Mr. Lopez reminded me of Edward James Olmos, only with better skin. He had his arm around a woman who must have been Rio's mother, 'cause I know from Liza that she's White. Mrs. Lopez was crying all the way to the door.

Liza walked up to Rio and his parents. We all rose to follow her. "Get away from my son, it's all your fault," said Mr. Lopez.

"What do you mean?" said Liza.

But they just continued walking. Not even Rio turned back to hug her or say he'd call her later.

Liza started to cry. We banded around her like a Sistah Circle, trying to block out all the negative energy. I kept trying to bite back the tears that wanted so badly to flow. I was really afraid that Liza may have gotten herself into a situation that might be irreparable. But every time a bad thought passed through my mind, I replaced it with a good one. Like the time in elementary school when Liza spent the night at my house, and we tried to fix each other's hair. Only she has this straight, thin White girl hair and I have curly, kinky, Black girl hair. I pulled out my hair grease and applied it to Liza's hair. I put so much grease in her hair, it took an entire month for it to all wash out. She looked like she had a greasy Jheri Curl, only her hair was straight. And then Liza put the hot iron to my hair and practically burned off half the hair on my head. The kids at school laughed at us both for weeks, even when we tried to cover our heads with hats.

"Liza Ortiz," said the nurse.

We all walked over with Liza.

"Only one of you can go in with her."

Liza grabbed my arm and pulled me along with her. The nurse led us into the doctor's office. We took a seat across the desk and waited for the doctor to come. Liza just sat cracking her knuckles. And I just bit my cuticles.

"Whatever happens, Liza, I will be right by your side."

The doctor opened the door. She was really tall with long jet-black hair and a very welcoming smile. She took a seat.

"Hi, Liza, I'm Dr. Chin."

She looked at me. So I quickly introduced myself.

"I'm her friend, Mariposa. I'm here for moral support."

"Liza, you're okay with her being here, to discuss confidential information?"

"Yes."

Dr. Chin smiled and looked to Liza with such motherly affection. "Well, we're here for two things: one, to talk about your options regarding your pregnancy, and two, to discuss your test results."

"Um-huh."

"So, what do you want to do?"

"I've been talking to Mrs. Matthews, and I think I want to keep the baby," Liza said.

I have to admit I was scared by the consequences of her answer but not surprised.

"Are you sure? Whatever you do is your choice, I'm only here to give you options."

"Well, Mrs. Matthews said I could stay with her and she would help me out since my family doesn't live in the safest part of town."

"Liza, how are you going to finish school and build a life?" I said.

"It's my choice, Mariposa. And you said you would support me no matter what. I love Rio, and this is our baby."

What could I say? It was her body. But once again I felt helpless with Liza. I could beat myself up about would've, should've or could've, but in the end, I had to respect her decision.

"Well, in that case, here is some literature about prenatal care and different birthing options. The clinic works with the hospital and since your family receives assistance, Medicaid will cover the expenses."

"That's it? You're not going to tell her about other options? Like an abortion?"

"Since we receive public funding, I can't advocate either way. I have to remain neutral. But I do understand your concern, Mariposa."

I kept hoping that Liza would at least ask about other options. It became clear that Dr. Chin could not volunteer any information as it would seem as if she was influencing Liza's decisions, which is messed up because she's only fifteen, and Liza could really use some advice.

"Well, I'll say it. Liza, your boyfriend is a batterer. He needs help. Do you really want to bring this baby into the world knowing that Rio will not be able to do anything to help you? He didn't even talk to you as he walked out."

"I know he loves me, Mariposa. And once the baby is born, he'll come around," said Liza.

"Fine, mess up your life," I said, slamming myself back against the chair.

"Liza, if you change your mind, my number is on the literature," said Dr. Chin. "Feel free to call me."

"Thank you," said Liza as she put the mounds of paper Dr. Chin gave her into her purse.

"Now, let's talk about the test results," said Dr. Chin. I quickly got over my anger and squeezed Liza's hand. Dr. Chin opened Liza's file. "Your tests all came back negative."

"Yeah!" I said jumping out of my seat.

I looked at Liza, and she looked relieved too. I was so happy that Liza didn't have another thing to worry about. Between Rio and the baby, she already had enough. I really thought it was gonna be serious after Rio and his parents snapped at Liza. That got me wondering what they were talking about.

"Now you know this means you're a very lucky girl. And from now on you're gonna what?"

"Use condoms and birth control," said Liza.

"And I want you to go through a safe sex series that we offer here at the clinic to educate young, sexually active people like yourself. Next time you might not be so lucky. You must learn how to protect yourself."

"Yes, I understand, Dr. Chin," said Liza.

"Great. Then we check in two weeks from now. Make sure you stop by the receptionist to make an appointment before you leave."

"Thank you."

As we left, Liza did as instructed and made an appointment. I walked back to the waiting room to find Sadie and Evita, still being all gushy with each other. They looked so cute and happy. It's funny how the most controversial couple in my life was the healthiest. I'm sure they'll have their drama at some point, but something tells me that Sadie and Evita will be able to deal with it.

They finally noticed me and jumped up to get the scoop. "She's clean."

Liza walked into the waiting room and we all jumped up and down around her.

"So when are you going to the abortion clinic?" asked Sadie.

The joyful moment scratched to a stop. Sadie didn't even know that it was her mother who convinced Liza to keep the baby. Mrs. Matthews is a great woman. She's just very pushy with her beliefs.

"I'm going to keep the baby."

"Are you serious?" said Evita.

"Yes."

"And guess what, Sadie? Your mom has volunteered to help her," I said.

"Liza, you didn't let my mom brainwash you into doing anything you didn't want to, did you?"

"No, Sadie. Your mom just helped me in making a decision that was best for me," said Liza.

"When is she going to learn to keep her nose out of other people's business? Are you sure, Liza? 'Cause my mom can be very convincing. I'm sorry if she was too much."

"No. I really feel like the baby will probably help him change."

"Liza, you know that if you stay with Rio, my mother will never allow you to stay at her house," said Sadie.

"Well, then Rio and I will just have to get a place together," said Liza.

"You're crazy, Liza. You know that, right?" said Evita.

"Maybe. But I know I'm supposed to have this baby," said Liza.

"Do you, Liza?" I said. "I gotta respect that, but if Rio ever puts a hand on you again, I swear, I'll kill him."

"Ditto," said Sadie.

"Me too," said Evita.

And we all put our arms around Liza. We exited the clinic, Sadie and I on either side of her and Evita walked in front, protecting the baby from whatever may cross Liza's way.

CHAPTER 20

REAL LOVE

I was bummed that Liza wouldn't be able to participate in the show, but hearing that Rio got kicked out of Stanford because Liza's brother made her press charges for his abuse made my day. He came to pick up his things with his parents and was then escorted out by Mrs. Hillaire. Rio hasn't returned any of Liza's calls. His parents have forbidden him to see her again and he claimed that Liza's baby wasn't his, which is a total lie. What a jerk. I just keep hoping every day that Liza would come to her senses and abort the baby. But I'm not keeping my fingers crossed.

I emptied all my homework for the week out of my locker and put it into my bag for the weekend. I needed to get home to prepare myself for the show tonight, so I marched down the hallway trying to put everything behind me.

When I reached the exit to the school, there was Ezekiel standing there waiting for me. Great. Just what I need. Here I am trying to move on and who shows up?

"I did it, Mariposa," said Ezekiel.

"Did what, EZ?"

"I broke up with Jessica."

"You what?"

"We're not together anymore."

EZ and Jessica finally broke up and honestly, I didn't have any reaction. After everything that had happened in these past months, I had come to terms with the fact that he would just be with Jessica, that maybe he and I weren't meant to be together.

"I told her I couldn't be down with her anymore." He moved in closer to me. "Will you go to Stern Grove, so I can explain everything?"

"No, I gotta get ready for tonight."

The old me would have dropped everything to be with EZ. Now I felt stronger and more disciplined.

"Please," said Ezekial, with a pout that was so hard to resist.

"I can't, EZ. I need some head space away from school so I'll do well tonight."

"Mariposa, c'mon, lend a brotha your ear. Pretty please."

I was going to walk off, but given all that EZ and I have been through, I felt he at least deserved an ear. A part of me was also curious about what he had to say after all these weeks since we kissed and he got back with Jessica.

"All right, but only for a few minutes. And not Stern Grove. Let's talk outside."

"Whatever you say."

So I walked to the beautiful eucalyptus tree that soared over our school and set my bag down to give EZ my full attention.

"So, what happened?" I asked.

"I realized that being with Jessica was really about caring too much about my street cred and pissing my mother off. I dated Jessica because I knew my mother would never approve. My mom thinks I'm the rebel, but it's Sadie. She's the one who remains true to her heart. It's just my mother can't know about Sadie because she could never deal with it."

"Okay."

"Well, when I kissed you, it felt like magic. Being the cool brotha I am, I couldn't tell you. So when I found out you kissed Sadie, that helped me play it safe."

"You just ignored me, EZ. I felt terrible kissing you and your sister. I was so confused. I didn't know if I was straight or gay. And at some point, I just stopped caring. I just let myself be."

"I want to be with you, Mariposa."

"We'll have the summer, and then you'll be off to college. You're not going to want to be with me then."

"I've loved you since the moment I saw you at camp," said Ezekiel.

"This romantic, wear-your-heart-on-your-sleeve stuff really does run in your family, doesn't it?"

"Mari, I love you. Don't you get it?"

"No! It's too late, Ezekiel. It's all about working on myself now, and not arranging my life so that someone else is happy. I don't have room for anything other than friendship."

"Fine. If that's all I can get from you, then it'll have to do."

I stood there thinking I would push him away. It didn't work. I didn't know where to go from here. I was getting used to the fact that maybe I needed to be alone. Frankly, I needed to focus on my performance tonight and that was what was most important.

"Ezekiel, we met as friends. We do friends well. Let's just keep it there. Nothing more, nothing less."

"If that's what you want, I'm cool."

EZ turned around and walked away. I knew he wasn't cool. It took a lot for him to tell me what he did, but it's not where I wanted to be right now. There were too many things rolling around in my head. And I needed to be true to myself.

CHAPTER 21

THE TALENT SHOW

On the night of the talent show, I was ready to perform. Sadie and Evita were in the dressing room getting ready. And I felt great knowing that all the people that I loved were out there waiting to see us perform. Jessica was out there rocking the audience. I could hear the crowd roar. But I really didn't want to focus on the spectacle she created tonight. It was about me focusing so that I could go out there and make myself proud.

There was a knock on the door. I'm sure Jessica was done because I could hear the crowd scream and clap. I took a real deep breath. I grabbed Sadie's and Evita's hands.

"For Liza," I said.

"For Liza," they both repeated.

We walked onto the stage in our red PUMA sneakers, jeans and hoodies with the *Sista Hood* across the chest. Liza was in the front row massaging her stomach and sitting with her brother on one side and Mrs. Matthews on the other. My mother, who looked sober and proud, sat next to Mrs. Matthews, cheering loudly for us all.

Ezekiel sat off to the side. I thought he would mean mug me, but instead he blew me a kiss. And for the love of friendship and struggle, I blew him one back. I didn't feel hard or like I had to prove anything to anyone. And it felt good.

Then to the left of Ezekiel, I saw Missy Elliott. And my heart started to pound with excitement.

We each took our place on the stage, Sadie and I in front and Evita in the back with her turntables. Sadie and I grabbed our mics and Evita gave us a beat.

I stepped up and looked out at my audience. And I'm not kidding, I felt this natural high. It was like this energy pulsated through my body, and I was ready.

"I'd like to thank everyone for coming out to support tonight. We'd like to give a special shout-out to Missy Elliott. Our families. And our ancestors. And this show tonight is for our girl, Liza, and her future.

"Okay, mic check," I said. Then I put my heart into launching what would hopefully be a winning performance.

Watch the picture that I paint like Picasso,
On the microphone you know I'm a diablo.
Leave it smoking like a cigar, on the stage I'm a star.
Turn the page, here we are and we are taking it far,
In this hip-hop game, props to the legends that came
before.
Now it's our time to kick in the door,
Got the crowd screaming feening for more.
From the rich to the poor,
No question what we doing this for.

The sistahood is in effect, mic check,
In the hood we get respect.

The sistahood is in effect, mic check,
In the hood we get respect.

My verbs and verses, I don't rehearse this,
A God-given gift meant to uplift.
Homie, enlist in my mental revolution,
Clean away pollution, rewrite the Constitution.
The world needs a new solution, come together find a
resolution.
Don't let them misguide you, hold your head up high
And keep it true, old school like the kicks with the kan-
garoo
Me an' my crew this is just how we do.

We finished and the crowd was hollering. Ezekiel and Missy Elliott stood and folks actually gave us a standing ovation. We all hugged one another and pulled Liza onto the stage to share our joy. We were so happy, we didn't even care if we won or lost. I had done my best.

My Mami was in the audience telling everyone, "That's my daughter. She takes after me." And then she did the unexpected—she put her fist in the air in salute to the Sista Hood.

Even Mrs. Matthews was proud of Sadie as she jumped up and down with joy like she probably did in church.

Missy took the stage with Ezekiel.

"And the winner of the 2005 Stanford High talent show, is . . ." said Missy Elliott. Ezekiel passed her the envelope for her to open. "The Sista Hood! Can you three amazing ladies come join us on the stage, please?"

The three of us headed to the stage with Liza to accept our award with pride. The positive energy in the audience was contagious and I felt so proud to be standing there with my sistas, feeling empowered and determined.

"These three, I mean four, young women will be joining me in Los Angeles this summer for my first ever Hip-Hop Leadership Camp. They will be taking classes with industry professionals and will have the opportunity to actually cut an album by summer's end. Congratulations, ladies."

I hugged my crew. Then I hugged Missy. Everyone was all happy. Ezekiel approached me and tried to give me a kiss on the lips, but I opted for the friendly cheek. Maybe in time I'll be ready, but for now I needed to just allow myself to be a girl and not always feel like I gotta be grown. However, the highlight of the evening for everyone, especially Mrs. Matthews, had to be the long lip-lock Sadie and Evita shared on the stage in front of the entire school. Mrs. Matthews just up and fainted right there in the front row. But that story is best left for another time.

ACKNOWLEDGMENTS

Mil gracias to:

My partner, lover and best friend—Alex Ramirez. As you now realize, creative people are blessed chaos that eventually find balance. Thank you for standing beside me with unwavering confidence and supporting me in actualizing my dreams.

My birth family—Elva, Tiffany, Justin, Chuck, Diana, Andy, Tony, Jodi and Nana—who love and support me no matter what I do. Especially my mother, Elva, whose strength and courage give me hope that anything is possible. And my grandmother, "Nana," who was my second mother when the world was too heavy for my mother to carry. To my sister-in-law Claudia, who ventures toward her own dreams, which I know she will find. To my mother-in-law, Luz, who loves deeply, know that you are loved too. To my niece Abby, for inspiring me with your intelligence, strength and courage.

Sofia Quintero, aka Black Artemis, who supported, loved and believed. Your sistahood has often given me the courage to soar in life, love and career. Your radical spirit has made this creative path we travel far less daunting. Here's to our next cofounding venture, Sister Outsider Entertainment. Your sistahood is truly inspirational.

To Ria Grosvenor, one of my oldest and dearest friends, who has transcended beyond friend to that of family, thank you for opening your home and providing me with the unconditional refuge and support to finish this book.

My Sista Warriors at Chica Luna Productions—Auro, Sone Sol, Sone Boogs, Mari and especially Black Artemis. For Karly and Ana, who had the courage to step up their leadership so that I could write and grow as well. You two are very loved. Word up to all the F-Word Chica Lunatics (Nyoka, Courtney, Desiree, Yahaira, Toni, Angelique, Patty, Shayla), as well as our interns—Lares, Mark and Jasmin. You all give me hope. And to the extended Chica Luna family whose dedication to social justice facilitates a place for not only their own art, but makes room for other women too—Martha Diaz, Tania Cuevas-Martinez, Erica DelaRosa, Anneleise Paull, Carmen Rivera, Susana Tubert, Martha Mas Ferrer, Lisa Smith, Cristina Kotz-Cornejo, Myla Churchill, Hillary Ureña, Kathia Almeida, Marilyn Torres, Sara Contreras, Aleeka Wade and Marcela Landres.

To my agent, Jennifer Cayea, whose confidence and relentless advocacy allowed me the space to become a better writer. I look forward to many collaborations to come.

To Tina Bartolome and Patty Dukes for your lyrics, which have added a voice to this book that makes it magic. You both got next.

To the Culture Club—Nicole, Norma and Lolita— that sets the bar for all sistahoods to come. Valeria Wilson, who I always carry in my heart, though distance gets in between our own sistahood. And to Lilliann Jìménez, Iris Morales and Dylcia Págan, who have provided me with an abundance of inspiration, courage, support and mentorship.

Teresita, Tina B, Sofia, Alex, Stacey, Marta and my Chica Luna sisters, for being great readers and providing me with invaluable feedback.

Shirley and Edgardo Miranda-Rodriguez at Somos Arte, for always being real and true to the movement.

A special kudos to Karly Beaumont (an amazing artist in her own right) who, next to my partner, family and close friends, has supported me the most with her steadfast assistance in making sure this book was a success at every juncture, from my own writing to web design to the production of *Sistahood: On the Mic*, the music CD. And a special shout-out to Miki Fujiwara at Urban Envy who has done an amazing job at designing the website for this book, which can be found at www.thesistahood.com.

To organizations and people who continue to create space for artists who have been traditionally invisible— Beth Janson and Tribeca All Access, the National Association of Latino Independent Producers, Paul Robeson Fund for Independent Media, Astraea Foundation, Frederick Douglass Creative Arts Center, the New York International Latino Film Festival, Harrison Reiner, Miguel Tejada-Flores, Mauricio Rubenstein and Marilyn Atlas.

To all the women who are not just true to hip-hop but continue to be true to themselves and Da Sistahood. May your light continue to shine.

To my *bisabuela*, Maria "My Esperanza" Valentin, whose wisdom, love and courage have always given me hope and vision. Though you are no longer physically on this earth, I still feel you walking with me.

Last but never least, the team at Atria Books at Simon & Schuster that took a chance on a new Latina writer and worked diligently to make this novel a success, especially my editor, Johanna Castillo. Your commitment to the Latino community and for developing new writers will eventually change the face of publishing. *Mil gracias* from the bottom of my heart.

AUTHOR'S NOTE

To download music featured in this book, go to
the music section of TheSistaHood.com and
enter code: MCPATRIA415.